Deborah

Prophet and Prayer Warrior

A Novel by
James J. Stewart

Prologue

My name is George Zuniga. My wife and I conceived Deborah after a New Year's Eve party in my home. God had prepared Alexandra and I for each other, which we have believed since the day we got engaged and on through this moment and beyond.

The previous Valentine's Day that year, God had set us up and brought us together under impossible circumstances. We both grew up in Long Beach, near Los Angeles, and we still do. We both went to Wilson High, but we hardly knew each other until we were in the same history class during our senior year.

On that Valentine's day, a Saturday, both Alexandra and her date, Steven Levitan, along with me and my date, Elyse Johnson, all happened to be at the Walt Disney Theater for a concert by the Los Angeles Philharmonic Orchestra. Both Elyse and I loved classical music. After the L.A. Philharmonic performed Debussy's *La Mer*, we went to the Lobby during Intermission. Elyse recognized Steven standing near the snack bar. "George, isn't that Steven Levitan?"

As I nodded, Steven looked towards us and asked, "Who called my name?" He saw Elyse. "Elyse? Is that you?" Steve and Alexandra walked towards us. "I didn't know you were into classical music." Their eyes locked.

At that moment, Elyse released my hand. "Both of my parents are in the Long Beach Symphony, Steven." Without another word, she put her arms around his neck and kissed him."

I think my mouth dropped open at that time. I glanced over at Alexandra, and her mouth was hanging open too. As we looked at each other, I shrugged. We just stood there with our mouths hanging open as Elyse and Steven continued to passionately kiss.

Steven looked at Elyse. "We can go to other concerts. Shall we get out of here?" She nodded. He looked at us. "My seats are among the best in the house, and Alexandra can show you,

George. Can you take Alex home for me?" I nodded. Steven and Elyse walked out together, holding hands.

I looked at Alex. "This is weird, isn't it?"

"It's beyond weird, George. We can at least enjoy the rest of the concert. Shall we use your seats or Steven's?"

"I cannot afford those expensive seats Steven bought, and it is a shame to let them go to waste. Still, I hate the way he's treated you, Alexandra. He didn't think to apologize to you for leaving you in the lurch."

She shook her head. "Elyse did not apologize to you either. Let's use your seats. I've been looking forward to hearing Tchaikovsky's 6th Symphony." When I held out my hand to escort her, she surprised me by putting her arm around me. "George, I'm glad you're willing to be my date. Maybe we can finally get to know one another before we graduate."

I was startled when she said "finally.' The rest of the concert was just as good as the beginning. After having some pie, a la mode in the Disney Theater café, I led her to my parent's Buick. We drove randomly around Southern California for several hours, and I took her out to breakfast at a *Denny's* before taking her home.

At her door, I had an inspiration. "I go to Ximeno Christian Church on Cherry near Anaheim. If you'd like to join me for worship tomorrow morning, we can have lunch afterward."

She put her hand on my cheek and kissed me lightly. "I'd love to, George. It's a date."

We dated twice that first week, including dinner the following Friday. We dated three times the week after.

After dating daily for just a few weeks, we got engaged on Easter Sunday. The following New Year's Eve, we drove to Las Vegas and said our vows at a tiny neighborhood church we had found on the Internet. We loved each other unconditionally and passionately then, and we still do.

Deborah was born nine months and three days later. The first time I looked into my daughter's eyes, I was in love. We have never called her Debby, always Deborah, and she was by far the loudest baby in the hospital's nursery.

We started reading the Bible to Deborah as soon as we brought her home from the hospital. She was happy, healthy, and strong. Once she was at home, she seldom cried except softly when she was hungry.

She was about a month old when we dedicated her at East Side Christian Church in Long Beach. I loved that old church at the corner of Seventh and Obispo. Behind the baptistry in that church was a stained-glass window depicting Jesus in the Garden of Gethsemane. As our pastor began the dedication ceremony, I kept glancing up into Jesus' face in the window. At that moment, I somehow knew that Deborah was going to make history and somehow glorify God.

Our daughter started walking when she was only fifteen months old. I couldn't have been prouder. Her red hair was longer, and her freckles remained few and faint.

From her earliest days of elementary school, Deborah got high marks. As she began adolescence, she was popular with the boys. She grew taller, and she was poised. Each time Alexandra took our daughter shopping, it was followed by a Daddy-Date night. Deborah's beautiful face and figure turned heads wherever she went, and I was a doting and protective father.

Highly intelligent, Deborah always spoke clearly and precisely. We let Deborah go on double dates beginning when she was a freshman at Wilson high school. She decided she wanted to buy an electric harp, so she began doing things to raise the money. It was expensive, but she purchased a thirty-three-string acoustic/electric harp in August before her junior year at Wilson High. She taught herself to play and began practicing two to three hours each day. She liked 'group dating,' particularly with couples from our church.

The first time she went on a single date, it was with her future husband, James Maffett. James asked her out the first time when we were at a church dinner, where she learned he was the son of a successful commodities trader who had recently moved to New York. James was living with an aunt and uncle. Our daughter's wedding to James was the day after they graduated from Wilson High. She was eighteen, and James was nineteen. He had just completed his first year as a music history major at Cal-State Long Beach.

Now you know the background, and the story can begin.

Chapter One
Few Noticed

On her twentieth birthday, Deborah started her prophetic blog, *What Lies Ahead*. She had already begun to think of herself as a prayer warrior. She was beginning to pray throughout the day. She also began to have prophetic dreams. George continued to be her proud Dad.

Our story begins, however, a few weeks after Deborah and James came back from their honeymoon in Grand Teton National Park. Each morning, before they got out of bed, Deborah and James read the Bible and prayed. During her music studies at Cal-State Long Beach, they had to set an early alarm for two hours of reading and prayer to begin their day before their first classes.

Almost every afternoon, if she had no classes, Deborah practiced on her harp for two to three hours. Without realizing how much at first, she began praying silently off and on throughout each day, even when she was playing with her quartet. Sometimes she silently prayed while music came through her hands from memory.

Her quartet was called *New Rocks*. It included a guitarist named Ted, a keyboard artist named Dick, and a drummer named Gary, with Deborah on her harp. After their first gig at Long Beach's *Petroleum Club*, they began to have rave reviews, getting them engagements nearly every weekend.

For Deborah, she was glad to get that financial relief for her parents. George worked hard, and Alexandra had some earnings from her artistic talents, but their total income was middle-class at best. By the end of her freshman year, the income from *New Rocks* engagements was completely paying for the educational expenses for all four of them in *New Rocks*, not just Deborah.

Very few people knew that Deborah was writing blog entries nearly every day because her blogs were recorded videos with a disguise. At a garage sale just after she and James got married, she had picked up a plastic mask of her favorite old-time actress, Audrey Hepburn. It was rather stiff, but it served her purpose. Deborah would read her blog while wearing the mask for recording it on her laptop's built-in camera and microphone.

Only James knew that she would write her blog entries after they prayed together each night or the next morning at the latest. He encouraged her to let her blog reflect her prayers. That was the first step in her becoming a prophet.

Making her video blog entries while wearing the mask meant she maintained her privacy and anonymity. She also securely bounced her blog entries through servers in six other countries on the Internet before they emerged on a server in Chicago that held her virtual private network.

At first, very few people discovered her blog because she did not advertise it. The few who saw her entries quickly became fans and subscribed when they recognized in the news that Deborah was a prophetess. A server service in Seattle handled collecting fees from her subscribers at a rate of one dollar a month or ten dollars a year.

Meanwhile, Deborah and her quartet were gaining more income from their engagements and from audio recordings that they offered for sale on Amazon Music. James was gaining an excellent reputation as an associate administrator for music programs at West Coast Christian College.

On his Facebook page, James posted how he was enjoying a new video blog that he had discovered called *What Lies Ahead*. Each time he thought one of Deborah's blog entries was particularly important, he would also mention it in a tweet on Twitter. That happened frequently. Sometimes he would forward one of her entries to Instagram. Her subscriber list began to grow week by week. The income didn't matter that much, but her subscribers seemed to further promote her blog.

After a dream one night, Deborah warned James. "In a dream last night, I saw your parents being put into an ambulance."

"Really!" He took out his phone and called them. "Good morning! We've not talked a week or two."

"Good morning, son! I was just getting ready to go to work. How are you and Deborah doing?"

"We're both doing well. Deborah had a dream last night, seeing you and Mom being put into an ambulance."

"Wow! That's unusual, isn't it. Living in New York, now, we hardly ever use our car. We take taxis and the subway everywhere. Don't worry about it. We're always careful."

The conversation continued for about a half hour. The next day, a domestic terrorist bomb went off that killed sixteen people, including his parents, as he arrived in front of the building where he worked. There were over a hundred additional people injured. The damage to the surrounding buildings was massive.

James and Deborah flew to New York for the funeral, and then they talked about it for days after they returned home. "I suppose this should have been easier because God warned us, but our losing my parents is excruciating!"

Deborah hugged him. "I know. I loved your Dad and Mom too. Even with our warning, though, they couldn't have seen this coming. You and I must let ourselves grieve. Grief never ends but does change. It is simply a passage and not a place where we stay permanently. It is not a sign of weakness or a lack of faith. It's the price of our love for your Dad and Mom."

James shook his head. "I know. I know." They hugged and wept together that day and for several weeks afterward.

The lawyer that drew up that will for James' parents flew out from New York to Long Beach to discuss it with them. There were some major shocks. As their lawyer opened his briefcase, he spoke quietly. "I knew them for many years. Your Dad and Mom did not tell you just how successful he was with his commodities trading. It was because they were intensely private people with everyone. I only learned about their successes when they had me draw up their will. They were proud of your success at West Coast Christian College, James. They were confident that your successes would multiply in the coming years."

He stopped to look directly at Deborah. "They loved you dearly, Deborah. They were looking forward to your giving them one or two grandchildren eventually."

She nodded. "I loved them too. James and I are going to start a family soon."

The lawyer reached into his briefcase. "They made bequests to each of you individually. Deborah, they left you a portfolio of stocks and bonds currently worth just shy of two hundred fifty million dollars."

Her mouth dropped open as she stared at him. "You're not serious?!"

He nodded his head. "I am." He paused. "James, you have inherited the remainder of their estate." He handed James a folder. "You'll both need to hire an investments firm to manage all this. On the current market, your portfolio, James, is worth more than a billion and a half dollars."

James reacted as Deborah had. He thought he knew his Dad, but this fortune was beyond money to Him. The lawyer remained while they discussed all the implications. He recommended a local law firm, Houser and Beam, before he left that evening. He flew back to New York the following morning.

After they ate some dinner, Deborah and James knelt at the foot of their bed and prayed for more than two hours. Overnight, God gave Deborah a dream of an investment firm that both she and James could use.

They started making new plans based upon their prayers and their new financial status. They prayerfully hired Houser and Beam as their lawyers, and they hired the investment firm in her dream. They sold their house in the Los Altos neighborhood of Long Beach and moved into a much larger home on Signal Hill. It's a little two square mile incorporated community that rises nearly a hundred fifty feet above the ocean. It is surrounded by Long Beach.

A private security firm began to monitor their new home. James began posting Twitter and Facebook entries regularly about Deborah's blog entries in *What Lies Ahead*. That boosted her visibility and subscriptions. Deborah's posts were important, but James had gained increased popularity himself. He began to gain a new reputation as a philanthropist with his inherited wealth.

They made an appointment with Pastor Jerry for a Tuesday morning. James explained what had happened carefully. "When my parents were killed in that terrorist explosion in New York, Deborah and I inherited substantial investments they had acquired. We are not going to give a full tithe to the church. In addition to what we give to the regular budget, we're establishing a fund for our missionaries and church-related causes. We want you to know that when emergencies arise, please feel free to ask. Also, we're also making a gift to your IRA."

"Thank you! You're both very generous."

They went on to talk about James' parents and their plans to start a family.

At that point in their married life, Deborah's prophetic blog posts had only a limited number of followers and subscribers. She didn't mind because they had ample financial resources.

On their fifth wedding anniversary, James and Deborah went out to dinner. They invited her parents, Alexandra and George Zuniga, to join them at the Black Angus restaurant. After they had placed their orders for prime rib, George was curious and spoke softly. "We've been watching your blogs every day, Deborah. Over at our church, someone had asked us if they had seen a blog called, *What Lies Ahead*. The first time we watched and heard it, we knew it was you."

Alexandra nodded. "What cinches it for me is your voice behind the mask. The mask is a nice touch. I think you've collected every Audrey Hepburn movie she ever made. You even acquired a poster of her when you were fourteen. You and James had a framed when you got married. I assume you still have that somewhere. I know that you got that mask at a garage sale. I hope you can get a better one though."

George smiled. "We're proud of you both, and we're delighted with the blossoming of your faith. Does your blog grow out of the two of you praying together?"

Deborah nodded and spoke as softly. "Yes, but let's not discuss it here." She began to speak in a normal tone of voice. "Dad, you've got lots of business contacts, booth in Alexandria and at the Pentagon. Do you think that the political corruption in Washington has gotten worse?"

"Definitely." George paused. "Money, sex, and power motivate most of the political establishment, and there's sadly too few exceptions. There are many wicked people in our nation's capital that corrupt the government. Why?"

Deborah was now profoundly serious. "Do you remember a news item just over a year ago, when a hacker named Jethro Underwood put the intelligence agencies into a panic?"

"Of course! He broke past the firewalls of just about all the computers in the Washington beltway and offered, simply as a patriot and at no charge, to fix their security problems. He did, and no criminal charges were filed against him. There's rumors that he was hired to do monthly security checks for them."

Deborah nodded. "Jethro is an intensely private man, and virtually no one knows where he lives. Last week, God opened a door for me. God helped me send a message to Jethro past all his personal security measures that no one else has been able to breech. He's asked to meet with me tomorrow morning, and God is putting us in a private dining room on the Queen Mary." She paused. "Here's our salads."

Their waiter rolled a cart to their table and served them their salads and bowls of soup. They did not speak again until the waiter left.

Alexandra was as curious as George. "Who made the reservation for the dining room? Did you? The Queen Mary Hotel is a great tourist attraction, and George and I have had dinner there a couple of times."

Deborah smiled broadly. "No, I didn't, and Jethro assures me that he didn't. I had a vividly colorful dream last night in which a man dressed in white escorted us to where we would eat. Psychologically, dreams are typically in black and white. When I have a dream in full color, I know that Our Lord is providing it. The meeting that we are going to have was not in the dream. As we left the little room in the dream, both our escort and the door behind us disappeared. I woke up to my cell phone alarm."

George laughed softly. "When God provides dreams, they sure can be memorable." He looked up. "Here comes our waiter." He smiled. "May I assume you're going to tell us more about that dream and about the meeting?"

Deborah nodded. "Someday. Not today."

The rest of the anniversary dinner went smoothly. Deborah and James told her parents some of the details of their inheritance from James' parents, but not the amounts. They talked about their new home on top of Signal Hill, looking over its eastern and southern slopes. After dessert, James and Deborah took her parents up there to their home and played bridge until after midnight.

At 8:00 sharp the next morning, Deborah and Jethro arrived at the Queen Mary Hotel, and their escort, dressed all in white, took them through a lounge to a dining room just like the one in Deborah's dream. As their escort left, sliding doors between the lounge and the dining room closed silently behind them and almost disappeared.

The hacker looked across the table. "It's nice to meet you, Mrs. Maffett. I've been reading your blog for a couple of months. You are the only person who has ever gotten past all my security with your email. Do you mind telling me how you did it?"

"Call me Deborah. I'm a woman guided and empowered by prayer, Jethro. Since we're going to be on a first name basis, I won't call you 'Mr. Underwood.' The day I sent that email, I saw things happening on my laptop's screen, without my touching my keyboard or trackball. Then a messaging form opened on my display. I wrote you the message that I felt spiritually inspired to write, and then I clicked send. My screen went blank for a moment, and then my browser window re-opened at its home page."

Jethro drank some coffee. "I tried to trace your email, but after bouncing around to several countries, it went to a relay on Mars and disappeared."

Deborah laughed. "Mars? God does everything well!"

He had a startled look. "God? I'm sort of a marginal Christian, at best. I don't go to church very often. I'm glad God did that, because now I know another place where people trying to trace me can have me disappear from them."

Their entire reality seemed to blink, and breakfast appeared in front of them. He looked at his plate in front of him. "Steak-and-eggs is by far my favorite breakfast, but I hardly ever have it, and nobody knows it's my favorite breakfast but me."

Deborah nodded. "Known by you and God. A waffle with bacon, with ripe honeydew on the side like this is my favorite breakfast. I seldom fix it for my husband and me." She paused and looked up. "Thank you, Lord!"

"Amen! Thank you!"

"I might as well tell you about why I wrote to you as we eat." She ate some bacon and a forkful of waffle. "God wants you to clean up the corruption in the Washington Beltway. Beyond that, God wants you to clean up state government corruption as well. Use all the Internet resources available to you. If you do everything God's way, on His terms, and according to His perfect timing, the results will last more than two generations. God will be glorified."

Jethro put his fork down. He took a deep breath, and then he sighed. "Mrs. Maffett – Deborah. I know I'm good. I like to think I'm the best. It may well be that I'm as good as I think I am only because God guides and empowers me. Still.... I've got to think."

Deborah nodded. "When you fixed the security holes in all those Beltway computers, I believe you installed hidden back doors in all of them, didn't you?"

He swallowed. "Somehow, I doubt that's a lucky guess on your part, so we can both assume that all the geeks employed by their respective agencies have searched out at least some of those back doors, although I'd like to think that they haven't found all of them."

She smiled. "Don't you think that God was guiding you and helping as you install those hidden back doors?"

"I suppose."

"God is our shield and fortress, so none of those back doors have been found. God never makes mistakes, Jethro."

"That sounds interesting, but how can that be always true?"

Deborah was thoughtful as she sipped some coffee. "The answer is actually simpler than you might think. Albert Einstein gave the best answer to the question way back in the last week of December in 1944, just before the end of World War II. In a poker game with the gambler called Nick the Greek and other gamblers, he said, 'God created time so that everything wouldn't happen all at once.' Think about it. Since God created time, He does not have to live within time's constraints as we do. It also means he's omnipresent."

"So?"

"In order to make a mistake, you must do something at one point in time, and then you look back later at what you did earlier to see the mistake. God is eternal – without time. He doesn't ever make mistakes."

Jethro was thoughtful. "That makes sense, but of course, no one can imagine life apart from, 'time's constraints.'" He paused. "Okay." He paused again. "Still, you obviously have a better relationship with God than I do. If God wants me to confront all the Beltway's corruption, I want you with me in those battles."

Deborah looked straight into his eyes. "If I do that, you must face the simple fact that you will never be able to take any credit for the corruption's collapse. A woman – not me – will be a sign of the end of all the corruption, and you will be only deep in the background, very deep."

Jethro nodded. "I can live with that. I like working in the shadows anyway."

"You may enjoy working in the shadows for now, but still another woman will bring you permanently out of the shadows, and you will be glad she did."

Deborah paused. "It would be helpful for you to give my blog some of your best security." She handed him a card. "That's the business card for my music group, *New Rocks*, with my personal email address and phone. That's enough, isn't it?"

He looked at the card and nodded. "Sure."

"Have you had enough to eat?"

He nodded. "I've had plenty." As they stood up, everything on the table disappeared, along with the table and chairs as well. He looked around. "Wow."

The doors slid open again to the lounge, and their escort was standing there, waiting for them. As Deborah and Jethro started walking, both their escort and the doors in the wall disappeared.

Deborah looked at Jethro. "Let me show you something." She pointed. "Look at the wall where the door into our dining room opened." He nodded. "Now step through that doorway to the left of where we ate and look in the direction of where we ate breakfast."

He walked over and took a step through the door to look. He looked inside again. Then outside again. His moth dropped open. "That dining room doesn't exist!"

She nodded. "God is at work with us, Jethro, and He will fight our battles with us." She smiled. "Pray about that too. When you have finished praying all this through, some plans will begin to form in your mind with details to completion. You and I will talk much more then, perhaps in a few months, I think."

"Do you believe I can plan this in a few months?"

She nodded. "With God's help – and only with God's help – you can." Deborah stopped by a railing. "You go ahead. You've got a full tank of gas, and that noise in your car's front end is no longer a problem. Go home."

Jethro was startled. "How did...?"

Deborah shook her head. "I don't know, Jethro, but God knows everything."

He opened his mouth to say something, but he closed it and started down a gangway. At the bottom, he turned, stopped to wave, and then, walking rapidly, he was soon out of sight.

She looked up, and the light around her seemed to fade into darkness. Countless stars began to twinkle even though it was mid-morning. A wondrous peace began to envelop Deborah, humbling her. She could sense God's presence and power acutely. "You're in control, almighty Yahweh. Yes, Loving Father you are." She sighed. "I don't know why you've chosen me, or why you're using me in this or any other way, but I trust you. I now understand the words of the prophet Habakkuk more clearly now, even though his language was in terms of his agricultural life."

> *Though the fig tree does not bud and there are no grapes on the vines, though the olive crop fails and the fields produce no food, though there are no sheep in the pen and no cattle in the stalls, yet I will rejoice in the LORD, I will be joyful in God my Savior.* [Habakkuk 3:17-18 (NIV2011)]

She stood there, enjoying God's presence, until a slight breeze began to blow, and daylight emerged again. It was getting chilly there in the Long Beach / San Pedro Harbor, and she knew that her husband James was already at work at the college.

In the parking lot, her car started easily. Driving out of the Queen Mary's parking lot, it did not take long to leave the harbor's islands and start going north on the Long Beach Freeway. She turned east on the Atlantic Avenue exit.

Her phone rang. The dash display said it was James. She touched a button on her steering wheel. "Hi, James! Everything went as expected. Again, God is amazing!"

"Where was the private dining room?"

"Actually, it doesn't exist."

"What? What do you mean?"

"A sliding door opened in an outside bulkhead, where there is nothing but a walkway on the other side. Instead, the doorway opened into a nice little dining room. There was no waiter. His favorite breakfast of steak and eggs simply appeared in front of him. In the same way, I got a waffle, bacon, ripe honeydew, juice, and coffee."

"Even though we've both already had breakfast, that sounds delicious."

"It was. When we got up to leave, everything left on the table disappeared, along with the table and chairs."

"Wow! As we like to say, 'God does everything well.'"

"Right. Jethro is going to need a few months for planning, I think. I hope my part will begin to unfold when I'm sleeping tonight. I assume you're already at work."

"Yes. Today I'm continuing my faculty search for next fall. Our current vocal music professor, Wayne Schmitt, is retiring this June."

"Right. I remember. Have you gotten answers to any of your queries?"

"So far, I've gotten about a dozen. The lists of the best vocal music professors in the country are each different. Each has different men and women on every list. Interestingly, one man's name appears on every single list. If other responses to our queries are the same, I know who I want to be our next vocal music professor."

"Right. I'm headed for home. I'll see you this evening. I love you."

"I love you too." They ended the call.

She was in their home atop Signal Hill in less than fifteen minutes. She backed into their garage, closed the garage door, and went up a few steps into their kitchen. She hung her coat up on a rack near the door.

Going into their great room, she went into their great room. While she and Jethro had been having breakfast, a bank of clouds had rolled in from the southwest, which were now filling the sky and obscuring the morning sun.

"Thank you, Lord, for my meeting with Jethro this morning. He seems like a good man. I hope he gains a better relationship with you as he takes on this huge task that you have given to him. Please help James make the right choice for the new professor of choral programs. I want to start a family with James, if that is your will for us. Deep inside, Lord, I'm wondering why I've not gotten pregnant yet. I trust you, Lord. I love serving you on your terms, your way, for your glory. You hold the future, so all praise and glory belong to you. Amen."

Chapter Two
A Fired-Up Internet

Deborah wrote her Friday night blog entry without being concerned it would be controversial. As images from her dream the previous night went through her head, her hands flew rapidly over the keyboard. She was maintaining her privacy and anonymity with Jethro's help, so upsetting the political establishment would not be a problem. This entry to her blog was several minutes long, and as she began, she simply spoke matter-of-factly.

> *Corruption in the Washington Beltway is going to end. God is at work. Some of the most corrupt individuals will move out of the beltway and fade into history's scrap heap. Some will repent and start to serve faithfully, getting them favorable reviews by future historians. Some will die.*

She gave examples from national news stories in recent years. It wasn't just Washington Beltway corruption that was addressed in this:

> *There is no corner that is so dark that God does not see. There is no whisper so soft that God does not hear. Corruption in lower levels of government will also end soon. The improved legal and spiritual health in all levels of government will last most of two generations, probably more. The financial health of our country's economy will vastly improve, and the number of those living in poverty and/or unemployed will be significantly reduced.*

In her last paragraph, Deborah offered hope.

> *All this does not have to be bad news for those who are corrupt and/or steadily pursue money, sex, and power. Scriptures confirm how many leaders accumulate God's wrath for themselves with their wickedness. God's judgment is sure and final. Any full-functional*

Christian knows, however, that God is gracious and merciful towards those who repent. As the Apostle John said long ago, God is love.

It got immediate and strong reactions, both positive and negative, from all over the country, all through the night.

Before noon, there were hundreds of responses to her Friday blog entry. By late Saturday afternoon, responses were in the tens of thousands. The most critical responses came from lobbyists and from members of the staffs of politicians. The week seemed to fly by rapidly. The biggest surprise for Deborah came the following Friday evening, when she learned that the subscriptions to her blog had gone up more than two thousand percent.

James was just as surprised as Deborah was. "This may mean that when we have our next national election just over a year from now, many of the incumbents will not be re-elected."

Deborah shook her head. "That doesn't seem likely. Let's not prematurely get our hopes up for that. Yes, all things are possible with God, but we have hoped for that in the past. The voting population has let us down. The voters tend to be fickle. As a result, we get the government we deserve even if it is not what we want. God is going to be winnowing our governments at all levels. When just the voting population acts to get rid of incumbents, changes tend to be temporary."

He nodded. "True. The Bible offers us plenty of evidence of how fickle people can be in comparison to the faithfulness of God. The Bible's books of Judges and Kings are prime examples."

Deborah smiled. "Things might get worse before they get better, and that may be part of my next blog entry." She paused. "Enough about my blog. Has God revealed to you another opportunity for us to use your Dad's wealth to bless people as we did last year?"

He shook his head. "Not yet, though I'm praying about that just as you are. This afternoon, I went over to the auditorium and listened to the weekly jam session. I've told you about the jam sessions before. It was a great change of pace."

"One of these days, I want to join you in listening in."

"I sat next to an interesting young woman who is a music major over at Cal- State Long Beach. Her name is Charlyn Koster. Between sets I learned that she's a talented musician, but she thinks she's going to pursue a career in journalism. You would like Charlyn, Deb. She's every bit as Christ-centered as you and I are. [*Elijah*, © 2020]"

"Add her to our prayer list. *New Rocks* has a gig this weekend out at the *Broadway West Dinner Theater* at Lakewood Center on both Friday and Saturday. I'll be rehearsing with them tomorrow afternoon and Thursday afternoon. I'll be practicing my harp a lot this week. Let's eat dinner out tomorrow, okay?"

"Sure."

Her phone rang, and her screen said it was Jethro. "Hey, Jethro, what's up?"

"Hey. On the Queen Mary I did not ask you about a budget. I think we'll need to hire some private detectives."

"Evidently, you've started praying, and that's excellent. I'll pray about this tonight and tomorrow morning. I suspect that God will want us to use detectives that are not based in our biggest cities. I'll call you tomorrow. Send any bills to the law firm Houser and Beam."

"Okay. There's no rush. Meanwhile, you should know that after your Friday's blog post, there were some attempts to hack into your computer. At our meeting on the Queen Mary, you asked me for some of my security measures. I didn't tell you that I had already taken care of that for you. I traced the attempted hacks to the F.B.I. and the D.S.A. or the Defense Security Agency. In both cases, I gave them a taste of my sardonic sense of humor."

Deborah smiled. "What did they find?"

"The F.B.I. hacker got wallpaper of the welcome screen of the main computer of the K.G.B. in Russia with the words,

"You've been Hacked." The Defense Security Agency hacker got a similar result on wallpaper of the equivalent computers in China. Both might possibly guess it was my doing, but they will never be able to prove it."

"Good. I'll share this with my husband, James. Shall I just text you with those detectives?"

"That'll be okay. We'll talk again soon." He ended the call.

Deborah told James about the call as they put their dishes in their dishwasher. Then they went into their home theater and watched a newly released comedy. It was after ten before they prayed and called it a night.

Just before dawn, Deborah had a dream. She found herself in Port St. Lucie, Florida, where she saw a storefront with a sign identifying a company called Drake Investigations. Her dream faded into the faces of several well-known Washington politicians. When that faded, Deborah found herself in Mentor, Ohio, where she was standing before another storefront identified as Wolfe Services. Then Deborah's alarm went off, and she and James began another day.

James was already out of bed and shaving at one of their two basins. "Good morning! When I got out of bed you didn't stir, so I decided to let you sleep."

She stretched. "That was a good decision. God gave me a dream just before the alarm went off. I've got two investigative agencies to pass on to Jethro. God is so good!"

He rinsed his face and grabbed a towel. "Let's read scriptures before we pray. I know you want to continue with our reading of John's gospel. I want to go back to the book of Judges in the Old Testament. I enjoyed reading about your namesake in chapters four and five. I want to go on from there and read again about Gideon."

"Okay."

Later, after they ate breakfast, Deborah dialed Jethro's number. He answered on the first ring. "Good morning, my friend. If you're calling me this early, God must have given you an answer to the question of investigative agencies."

She smiled. "This isn't early! I've been awake for more than three hours, and James is already on his way to work."

"Wow. You win. What have you got?" Jethro was business-like.

"I've got two for you. In Port St. Lucie, Florida, there's Drake Investigations. Port St. Lucie is on the state's east coast, a little over an hour and a half's drive north of Miami. The other one is Wolfe Services in Mentor, Ohio. Mentor is about a half-hour's drive east of Cleveland. Financing this will not be a problem. Bills, as I told you, are to be sent to Houser and Beam Attorneys in Long Beach. Do you need me to text you with this?"

"No, I've got it. I have hyperthymesia."

"That's life-long total recall, right?"

"Right. I'll keep you posted on my progress via our ultra-private email. Bye."

"Bye." They ended the call.

She looked up. "Okay, Lord, I guess that's one way you've equipped Jethro for this." She paused. "In my next blog, I think I'll talk about how, because you are eternal, you never forget." She closed her eyes. A blanket of warmth and peace enveloped her as she communed with God.

Over at West Coast Christian College, James opened another email response to his search for a new vocal music professor. Once again, one of the five names was Frank Schmitt. James touched his intercom button. "Julie?"

"Yes sir?"

"See if you can set up a video call with Frank Schmitt."

"Yes sir."

When the call went through about a half hour later, James was looking at a man in his mid-thirties. After their initial greetings, Frank calmly said, "A couple of friends of mine have told me that I might be hearing from you. I have never met your current vocal music professor, Wayne Schmitt, but he is a shirttail relative of mine."

"Really?"

"Yes! My grandfather Elias Schmitt and Wayne Schmitt's father were brothers."

"It seems vocal music talent and gifts run in your family."

Frank smiled. "It seems so. I've had a passion for vocal music, especially choral music, since I was a little boy."

James smiled. "That's excellent. I'm calling to offer you a full professorship of vocal music here at West Coast Christian College."

"I know you have an excellent music department there, but I think I must decline. Even if you were to offer to double my current income, the answer would be the same. My wife and I are happy here in Philadelphia. I only have a bachelor's degree, and if I were a full professor anywhere, I would be under constant pressure to get graduate degrees. You have a wonderful but large school there. The inherent faculty politics of a large school does not interest me."

James nodded. "I'd like you to consider this to be merely our first conversation. If I can guarantee that you would not be pressured to obtain an additional degree, would you reconsider?"

"I don't know. I'd have to pray about it."

James smiled. "Very well. I'll be talking with our Chancellor here, and I will get back to you in a week or so." They ended the call. James touched a button. "Julie?"

"Yes sir?"

"I need a half hour with Chancellor Wheeler as soon as possible."

"Okay."

James leaned back in his chair and closed his eyes. "Lord, thank you. I depend upon your guidance, as always." He paused. "I don't know him, but you do, and I'm sure he needs you. Please watch over him and watch over Frank Schmitt as mercifully and graciously as you watch over Deborah and me." James opened his eyes and went back to work.

At their home on Signal Hill, Deborah carefully read that day's blog script that she had written. Once again, she ran her grammar and spell checkers, and she again read through her script.

The doorbell rang. The front door's video camera feed appeared in a pop-up window on her computer's screen. It was the Fedex driver, so she went to the door and opened it. "Good morning, Jack."

"Good morning." He handed her his tablet, and she scribbled her signature. "Thank you."

"Have a blessed day, Jack."

He grinned. "I wouldn't want it any other way, Mrs. Maffett." He turned and walked back to his truck.

She took the package inside and shut the door. Quickly, she tore through the packaging and opened the box to see a new Audrey Hepburn mask. This one was more flexible and would cling to her face with a temporary glue that dissolves in perspiration or water. It had been custom-made for her by an artist in Reykjavik, Iceland, for Deborah and James' attorneys, Houser and Beam, who in turn had shipped it to her.

Going back to her script she added two sentences at the beginning. "Today I'm wearing a new Audrey Hepburn mask. I hope all you appreciate it." She rehearsed her script four times in front of a mirror. Then she recorded it on her laptop as usual. After double-checking the result, she posted it.

Ten minutes later, Jethro called her cell. "Deborah, I don't know where you got that mask, but it is amazing, and this blog entry is going to rattle a lot of political cages."

"That cannot be helped, my friend. Have you checked out Drake Investigations and Wolfe Services?"

"Yes. By the way, I have set up security for our phone calls, so long as our calls are between these two numbers. Fred Drake has a waiting list for his team's services, but when I told him what we would be doing he got excited. He said he had been praying for an opportunity to go after Beltway corruption. Anybody I give him to go after, it will have top priority."

Deborah smiled. "What about Saul Wolfe and his services?"

"Wolfe's fees are much higher, but he says he'll look forward to tackling what he calls 'this thorny problem,' as he puts it."

"Excellent."

"Deborah, every time I think about our encounter with that angel at the Queen Mary Hotel, I feel like praying. Maybe it is that angel stirring me up inside, I don't know, but I think I've spent more time in prayer since our breakfast together than in all my years before."

"It's a good habit to have. The Apostle Paul tells his readers to pray without ceasing. For me, that means living my life with a constant sense of God's presence and power."

"That sounds logical. There's one more thing. I certainly hope that we can trust your attorneys, Houser and Beam."

"We can. You mentioned my new Audrey Hepburn mask at the beginning of this call. An artist in Reykjavik, Iceland made the mask and shipped it to Houser and Beam. They, in turn, sent it to me."

"You actually look like the late actress in all the pictures I can find on the Internet. If not Audrey Hepburn herself, you could be one of her descendants with that mask. The mask conforms to your face perfectly. Is it glued on?"

"Yes, and it is a water-soluble and flexible glue. Are you familiar with a website called *Political Nightmares*?"

"Of course. I have given both Drake Investigations and Wolfe Services the password I use for total access. The webmaster for that site is a close friend of mine, and I am one of very few people that has total access to that video database of public statements by politicians."

"Good. God has certainly equipped you well for what He wants you to do. Keep me posted."

"Of course." They ended the call.

She went to the steam room in the master bathroom. After removing her mask and rinsing it, she spent some of the afternoon responding to some of the responses to her blog and catching up on her email correspondence. The remainder of the afternoon she practiced on her harp.

The sun was getting low in the sky when Deborah lit the grill on their patio and began grilling spareribs. After James parked in their garage, he could smell the aromas and smoke coming from outside. He splashed some water on his face in the master bathroom, and then he started setting up the rest of their dinner, which was in one of their ovens. From their wine cooler, he selected a bottle of a California Cabernet.

Walking up behind his wife, James put his arms around her and kissed her neck. "This smells great! On the way home, I thought about our plan to start a family next year, but I hope you'll get pregnant before we have to consult fertility experts."

She put her tongs down, turned, returned his hug, and kissed him. "I don't think my getting pregnant will have any effect on what God has given me to do with Jethro. He called me to express his appreciation for my new Audrey Hepburn mask."

He handed her a glass of wine to match his own. "It came? How do you like it?"

"I love it! After dinner you'll have to see my blog. The mask goes on and comes off easier than I expected. I turned on the steam in our wet room, and it came right off with no problems." She turned and looked at the grill. "This wine tells me you've got everything else ready, so let's eat. I'll shut down the grill."

After holding Deborah's chair, James sat down and closed his eyes. "Thank you, for this food, Lord. You bless us far more than we deserve. We give you the glory and pray in Jesus' name. Amen."

"Amen." She bit into a rib. "Jethro said that today's blog would rattle political cages. Evidently, he was right. I've already had quite a few responses. He has talked with both private detective firms, and they'll work out fine."

"Good. I've made an appointment with Chancellor Wheeler for Monday morning. If we are to get Frank Schmitt as our new Professor of Vocal Music, the Chancellor and I are going to have to come up with some kind of special offer."

Chapter Three
Embarrassment versus Shame

It was 3:00 AM on Monday morning. Suddenly, Deborah was wide awake. She sat up in bed and turned on the light. She spoke softly. "James!" She reached across the bed and shook him.

"What?" He was groggy of course. "What's going on?"

"We've got to go to the panic room!" Deborah was emphatic. "Let's go! Now! God will defend us, but we must get out of here and fast! Let's move! We have not got much time!"

Going down the hall, James pulled a hidden latch in the bookcase, and it pivoted to reveal a chute. Deborah jumped into the chute first, and after a few seconds, James jumped. The bookcase pivoted back to its normal appearance. At the bottom of the chute, they landed on a pad. They helped each other up and went to a large desk with security video monitors.

Figures entirely dressed in black, from hoods to shoes, approached the doors on both the east and the south sides. A third pair forced open a seldom-used door into the garage on the north side to get in there. The burglars had made no sounds. A small flashing red light in the panic room told Deborah and James that the security firm watching the house had been alerted.

The figures dressed in black seemed organized as they quickly went through the house, checking every room before returning to the great room. A female voice asked intensely, "Okay! Now what? Their cars are here, so, where are they?"

A male voice spoke forcefully. "Maybe they have a panic room. It could be anywhere, and it might take an hour or more to find them if they are hidden. We'll have to come back."

At that moment, with James and Deborah watching and listening in the panic room, God acted. James' eyes grew wide, and Deborah's mouth opened silently, as the figures in black that they were watching on the monitors suddenly disappeared.

It was like they had not been there at all. Not one could be seen on any of the monitors.

James touched a button, and the cameras swept the streets downhill in all directions. The nearest car on the street was half a block away, and they knew that it belonged to one of their neighbors. He turned to Deborah. "All clear. God does everything well." He pressed the 'all-clear' button for the security company, and the light turned green. Going up, they walked through every room and looked in every closet. Then they went back to bed.

The next morning, after Bible readings and prayers, they fixed frozen waffles and bacon for breakfast in their convection oven. After serving their plates and pouring coffee, Deborah prayed a short blessing for the food. James turned on the monitor in the kitchen while they sat down at the counter. Using the monitor's remote, he scanned for local news and turned off the mute.

> *Early this morning, Long Beach's Shore Patrol picked up seven men and one woman, all totally naked in the ocean, splashing the water and yelling. They tried to resist arrest, but they were wrapped in blankets and taken to the Shore Patrol's lockup. KTLA's Jeff Oszoz recognized three of them as previously arrested members of the EX-20 gang, and all of them were held on outstanding federal warrants until the FBI comes to pick them up.*

James had a faint smile as he muted the sound. "I guess this is what happened to those people last night. That description sounds like it could be the eight people who broke in."

Deborah nodded. "It appears so. The water temperature right now along the Long Beach shore is just over sixty degrees. Brrr! That's too cold to swim without at least a wet suit! Praise God again, for being our shield and fortress!"

"Amen to that!"

Deborah finished off her juice. "What time are you meeting with the Chancellor this morning? Are you meeting in his office in the administration building?"

"Yeah. I'm first on his calendar for 9:00, according to his secretary. For starters, I want to offer Frank a full professorship at doctoral salary level. He'll need a guarantee of no further requirements for additional degrees. He'll still get raises based upon longevity. I want to make the offer as attractive as possible. What's up for you this morning?"

Deborah was thoughtful. "I'm feeling prompted this morning to go down to the church and pray in the sanctuary . I know I can pray here at home or anywhere, but this morning, that's where it seems I should go." She paused. "If you want to head for your office, I'll put the breakfast dishes in the dishwasher and wash and put away the frying pan."

"Okay." Getting off his stool there at the counter, he headed off to brush his teeth. Deborah got up and started loading the dishwasher. When James returned to the kitchen, they hugged and had a lingering kiss. "I'm holding a faculty meeting this afternoon, so I probably won't get home until nearly six."

"Okay. I'm fixing a Cornish hen with rice stuffing. Dinner time can be flexible."

He gave her another hug, and then he turned and went into their garage.

Deborah started the dishwasher, and then she headed towards their master bath before leaving for the church. Traffic was light, so it took just over ten minutes to get to Cherry Avenue near Anaheim, and Ximeno Christian Church.

Just inside, she stopped at the church office. The church's secretary was working at her computer station. "Good morning, Celia. I want to spend some time praying here this morning. Is anyone in the sanctuary?"

The secretary shook her head. "I'm holding down the fort until after 10:00, when some ladies from the Christian Women's

Fellowship are going to start fixing lunch in the basement for their monthly meeting. The sanctuary's all yours."

"Thanks!"

Walking in from the rear, Deborah saw the worship center awash with color, because the sun shining brightly through the stained-glass windows. "Thank you, Lord. I'm glad I've got good eyes to see and enjoy this morning's light and the wonderful colors." She knelt on the carpeted stairs near the front and began to pray. In the eyes of her mind, she saw buildings and people in Washington, D.C., and in the capitols of several states. She also saw images of people flying up and down to communications satellites. Through it all, she got a clear idea of what Jethro was trying to accomplish. Then she felt a tangible peace envelop her.

It was nearly noon when Deborah left the sanctuary and the church. She was hungry, so she drove west over to the Long Beach Mall and its food court. She parked and went in the entrance that was adjacent to the food court. Going to the May Lee Chinese Food station, she ordered some sweet and sour stir-fried chicken over steamed rice. As she was sitting down at a table, she looked up to see Jethro walking towards her.

He was grinning. "This is a surprise! I haven't been in this mall in months, and when I walk into the food court, here you are!"

"Hi! I'm having sweet and sour chicken over rice. Are you hungry?"

"I'll be right back." A few minutes later, he sat down across from her. "Is it possible that this isn't a coincidence?"

Deborah nodded. "I've spent most of the morning in prayer at my church over on Cherry near Anaheim." She lowered her voice slightly. "I saw images of people and places that concern us, and I saw you with a dotted yellow line connecting you to satellites."

"Do you often see images when you pray?

"No, not very often, but I often remember colorful dreams when I wake up in the morning. Countless authors have pointed out that God seldom speaks to Jesus' followers with audible words." She paused to eat a forkful of chicken and rice. "Most of the time, God speaks through actions. I'll tell you something now that you must absolutely keep under your lid, okay?"

He nodded, and she began to speak much more quietly. "Early this morning I awakened from a vivid dream, I sat up in bed, and I turned on the light. We have a panic room in our home. You probably do too."

"Yep."

"My husband and I went to ours, and on video monitors, we watched as our home was invaded by eight people dressed entirely in black and looking for us. While we were watching, James and I were shocked when those eight criminals suddenly vanished – totally disappeared. God is our shield and fortress." She paused to take another forkful of sweet and sour chicken. "You may have seen in this morning's news how the Long Beach Shore Patrol arrested eight naked people in the ocean this morning. They turned out to be part of EX-20."

He put his fork down, and his mouth hung open. "It was them?"

Deborah smiled. "I can only say for sure that there were eight burglars, and we heard a woman's voice as well as a man's voice. In the ocean at the beach there were seven men and one woman."

Jethro nodded. "That's good enough for me. Your church is on Ximeno?"

Deborah shook her head. "It's on Cherry near Anaheim. It used to be a few blocks north of Livingston Drive on Ximeno, but several years ago, we moved to its current location. That's eight or ten miles east of your home isn't it?" He stared at her, surprised. "Don't' let that bother you. In prayer I've seen you living in the Palos Verde Estates."

"Dear God!" he muttered.

Deborah nodded. "Yes, God loves us all. Wayfarer's Chapel is there in Rancho Palos Verde Hills near you. It is a small glass church built amid a grove of giant redwood trees. Even if you don't go inside the church, it might be a good place for you to pray there among the redwoods."

Jethro nodded. "I've driven past it a number of times." When they finished eating, he said he was heading to that chapel. Deborah headed for Signal Hill and her home.

Over the next several months, EX-20 gang members tried twice more to go after Deborah and James. Neither time they did not get inside the house. The first (second) time, the fifteen attackers ended up at Canon Beach, Oregon, where the water temperature was in the low 50s, with the air in the low 40s. The police at the little town of Canon Beach were easily able to subdue all of them because the criminals were so cold and violently shivering. They were simply turned over to the FBI within an hour because that small town didn't want to mess with an event like that.

In April, EX-20 tried again, but with twenty of them getting as far as James' and Deborah's driveway and their front yard. Darkness enveloped them, and the next thing they knew, they were asleep in the shadow of Uluru or Ayers Rock, in the center of Australia. Although they were naked and unarmed, they tried to put up a fight with local authorities. By sunset, soldiers had rounded up all twenty of them. It would take six months for any of them to get extradited back to the United States, but outstanding arrests held them there when they returned to the U.S. Deborah and James only saw the arrests in Australia on video.

About that time, Jethro bought a new server for his computers just to store the files he was building on the hundreds of politicians, lobbyists, and others being investigated for the confrontations project. All Jethro's computers and related equipment were in a secure room that did not exist in any of Los Angeles County's records.

Wolfe Services worked directly with Jethro, and Drake Investigations was more than happy to work under Saul Wolfe's leadership. In each file on Jethro's server there were videos from

Political Nightmares. Once confrontations would begin, alibies would be extremely difficult to create.

Deborah's video blogs continued to be controversial because they were filled with truth that few wanted to hear. Early one summer Sunday afternoon, Jethro raised a new issue during a video call one afternoon. "I'm seeing more and more instances where media producers and editors are intentionally supportive of corrupt people motivated by money, sex, and power. I'm wondering if we should simply involve them indirectly with the others, or should we confront them directly? I've been praying about it, and I'm not sure."

Deborah sighed. "I've been praying about this possibility too. All of us involved in this have to be extremely careful not to get our own hands dirty with any of this."

"Maybe someone already has, and you and I don't know it. At least, I don't. Do you?" Jethro was concerned as well.

"No, but I must humbly approach God about this. If I'm at fault, I need to own up to whatever I've done, even unknowingly."

"Is that possible?"

"Sure. We're all sinners, and we make mistakes. This is Wednesday. Let's talk again on Saturday morning."

"Okay." They ended the call.

Deborah looked up and closed her eyes for a few minutes. Opening them again, she pressed one of her speed-dial buttons. "Wolfe Investigations."

"This is Deborah Maffett. I'd like to speak to Mr. Wolfe."

"Just a moment." Deborah waited only a few seconds.

"This is Saul Wolfe, Mrs. Maffett. How may I help you?"

"Jethro and I suspect that someone working with us on this project has gotten our efforts stained by the corruption we are investigating by using some of the very tactics we deplore."

"I concur. Do you suspect anyone in particular?"

"No. You're highly intelligent as well as an experienced investigator. I'd like you to give this some serious thought, and I'd like you to pray about this as well, sir."

"I'm not a religious man, I'm afraid. I seldom pray."

He could not see Deborah frown because it was not a video call. "Forgive me, Mr. Wolfe. I need two to three minutes to pray."

When she closed her eyes, images flashed before her mind's eye, and she smelled an aroma she had not smelled since childhood. Her time of prayer lasted less than two minutes. "Mr. Wolfe, I believe that just outside your house on the west side there is a large and rather unusual species of eucalyptus tree, is there not?"

"I'm curious as to how you know this."

"The weather forecast for the greater Cleveland Ohio area calls for thundershowers after 9:00 PM this evening. A bolt of lightning will strike your eucalyptus tree at 10:15 this evening because God is God, and because our King, Jesus, has plans and a purpose for your life if you will follow Him. Jethro undoubtedly told you that I am somewhat passionate about doing things on God's terms, God's way, and for God's glory. I personally hope that after this, you will take praying more genuinely."

"You're serious about this?"

"Yes, sir. Tonight, you'll sleep with the aroma of eucalyptus filling your nostrils. We'll be talking again this Saturday, sir." Deborah ended the call. She looked at her analog wristwatch. Nodding, she went to the kitchen and started her preparations for dinner.

Just after 5:30, when James came into the kitchen from the garage, he smelled *Charcoal Duck* in the smoker. "Hi, beautiful! Dinner smells wonderful!" They kissed. "I'm so glad you got this duck recipe from the chef at that restaurant at the top of a hotel in Kansas City."

She smiled. It's a real blessing, isn't it?"

"Yes. Is there time enough before the duck is done for us to get a shower and freshen up before dinner?"

"Sure! It won't be ready for nearly an hour yet."

Later, as they sat down at their dining room table, Deborah told James about her conversation with Jethro and her subsequent conversation with Wolfe.

"So, God gave you a clear picture of what He's going to do for Wolfe?"

"Yes. Before that brief vision, I'd not even seen a picture of where Wolfe lives there in Mentor. Evidently, his house faces Lake Erie, and the eucalyptus tree is on the west side of the house. His tree is one of only two or three varieties of eucalyptus that tolerate Cleveland's cold winters. I looked up eucalyptus trees on the internet. Most varieties of eucalyptus don't tolerate frost well at all."

Long after James and Deborah were asleep, Saul Wolfe had his bedroom window open, letting in cool and fresh summer night air. The nearest streetlights were at least twenty-five yards away, and his own security lights were downstairs. He had heard thunder in the distance as he was getting ready for bed.

At 10:15, there was a deafening clap of thunder accompanied by a blinding flash, as a bolt of lightning struck the tree. A strong aroma of eucalyptus was filling Saul Wolfe's bedroom as he muttered, "Oh, My God!"

He inhaled a deep breath and sighed. His mouth hung slightly open, and his eyes were as wide as they had ever been. "Dear God in heaven! Forgive me!" He stood up, turned around, knelt on his bed, and put his face on the blanket. It was almost midnight when he got under his sheet and blanket. The aroma of eucalyptus filled his bedroom as he closed his eyes and fell fast asleep.

When his alarm went off, he dressed quickly. From time to time, he would look out the window, which was still open, and he could see the tree with a charred streak. He closed it before putting on his shoes. Downstairs, he climbed into his Jaguar and drove south rapidly towards TriPoint Medical Center, and to the Waffle House nearby. He had slept better than he had for as long as he could remember. After ordering enough food for two people plus coffee, he closed his eyes and prayed until his order was put on his table. He fully enjoyed every bite, even though he had eaten a similar large breakfast before. He felt stuffed.

His office was part of the Great Lakes Mall, and he walked in about ten minutes later than usual. "Good morning, Abby!"

"Good morning, Mr. Wolfe."

"I want to have everyone working on the Jethro Underwood case to come in for a meeting this afternoon at 3:00. We need to confirm that every single one of us has been totally ethical in this investigation, and that none of us has gotten our hands dirty. If anyone is unable to come this afternoon, tell them to come to my home this evening at 8:00."

"I'll get right on it."

Going into his private office, he turned on his computer. He did not break for lunch, but that was not unusual. The first to arrive for the meeting came at 2:50, and all those working on the case were there by 3:00.

After telling them about his conversation with Deborah, he told them what happened after he got ready for bed. There was stunned silence at first, and then they all started talking at once. After patiently listening for a couple of minutes, he put up his hand for silence.

"I have a friend who is a pastor, and I'm going to see him tomorrow morning. Abby, don't expect me before noon."

"Okay."

"Now." He sighed. "In our business, sometimes we play fast and loose with the truth to get the results we want. As I said when all this began, our work on all aspects of this case must be clean. The people we're investigating are corrupt, so we must stand totally apart from them and not get stained by their corruption. If anyone working on this case has done anything that is not totally above board, I need to know now." He looked around at all of them, and they looked at each other.

Abby cleared her throat. "When I was making the calls and sending texts and emails to set this meeting up, I told everyone that if they weren't clean, they could just withdraw from the case."

Wolfe nodded. "Yes. If you withdraw from the case, I'll pay you for the work you've done. I'll have one of the others double-check your work. On Saturday, I'm going to be in a secured video conference call with Deborah Maffett, Jethro Underwood, and Fred Drake. Our team needs to be discussing this issue, among other things. If you're going to withdraw from the case, tell Abby before you leave. I'll probably still use you for some future cases in case you're wondering." He paused.

"Our work on this case is almost done, and the files are quite complete. Confrontations will begin soon. Many will be embarrassed. Some will be ashamed. If we've done this right, many will experience both." He sighed. "That's all, ladies and gentlemen."

After all the operatives had left, Wolfe leaned back in his chair and closed his eyes. With no forethought, he found himself beginning to talk with God, but not about the case. He began reviewing his life since childhood and apologizing to God for things he believed had displeased our Heavenly Father. As he began to remember a few verses in the Bible that he had learned when he was a child, he ended the prayer. On a shelf high up in his office near the ceiling, he found the Bible his parents had given him when he was ten years old. He began to read.

Chapter Four
Confrontations Delayed

After James left for work on Friday, Deborah set up the conference call on the large video screen in their great room. She had already programmed her laptop to make the connections, and even Jethro's connection happened quickly. "Let's start with you, Fred. Did you have to let anyone go, or did anyone drop out because of our double-checking everyone's ethics?"

Fred Drake shook his head. "It was sad when one of my guys dropped out last Tuesday morning, but he was embarrassed to say that he had lied on a few occasions to get the information he wanted. That afternoon, a husband-wife team I use regularly started double checking all his work. By Wednesday noon they could report to me, and I believe we're all clear now at my end."

Deborah nodded. "Good. How about you, Saul?"

Wolfe smiled. "I'm proud of my crew. Sally, a woman I have employed for years, told my secretary she thought she had to drop out during these final days, but after Sally discussed it with me, I was able to determine that there weren't any ethical violations for me to report. I was relieved. Early this past Monday morning I became a Christian, and my discussion with Sally seemed to confirm what I had determined with prayer."

Deborah was smiling broadly. "All that God does, God does well! Excellent!' She paused. "Jethro, I want our project's server files to be accessible to all four of us starting today. Will that be a problem?"

He shook his head. "No problem. Just give me an hour to double-check the security provisions. Fred, someone at Homeland Security tried to hack into your computer last night, and a program I had set up locked up all his personal files for eight hours. My security did the same thing for you two weeks ago, Saul. All our files will be available for study within an hour."

Deborah nodded. "Good, Jethro." She paused. "Let's give ourselves two weeks to examine all our files for this project. All our phones and emails have high security, so let's talk with each other regularly. I want us to start the confrontations in two weeks unless problems arise. I don't expect any, but it is best to be sure. We must not have any leaks or warnings slip out. Saul, Fred, since your workers are all reliable, use any of them you deem appropriate to assist you in examining the files for flaws."

They both nodded. Jethro was looking down, but now looked up at his camera and screen. "All four of us now have access to the directories and files. Anyone assisting you will have to do so through your local secure private networks." He paused. "Early this morning, I got an inspiration – perhaps an answer to prayer. I'm running a couple of automated programs I've created. One of them is simply looking for duplicate files. That one will be done in the next hour. There will soon be a new directory called Duplicates."

Deborah was intensely curious. "What about the other program?"

Jethro sighed. "I hope I've not bitten off more than I can chew. The other program is the most complex searcher I've ever written. It is examining all the video and straight audio files we've collected. On the surface, it is looking for files involving the same people, using voice recognition. Then, when it finds such files, it is analyzing the dialogs digitally. That part may take several days. Any results will be in a new directory labeled Coincidences."

"Indeed!" Wolfe was enthusiastic. "I will never underestimate you, Jethro. If that program works, as I expect it will, you and I may become much better friends!"

Deborah nodded. "As I said a few minutes ago, let's stay in touch. We won't proceed with the confrontations until we're all confident in our results. Are there any final thoughts, anyone?" They shook their heads. "Very well. Blessings, everyone!" The video call concluded.

As usual, James got home from his office at West Coast Christian College just after 5:00 o'clock. Deborah was working her phone while sitting at the counter. In front of her were two wine glasses and an unopened bottle of Cabernet. She stood up, and they embraced. After kissing him she said, "It's been a long week, and it is Friday. Let's eat out this evening."

"Okay. Shall we enjoy some wine first?"

"That's why I put out the glasses and bottle. Let's drink it in the love seat by the front windows." While he opened the bottle and poured, she continued. "The video call went fine. We are going through all the files we've accumulated over the last several months. Then there'll be two additional files, and I have no idea how long it will take to work our way through them."

After she filled James in on the rest of the conversation, he was thoughtful. "When you and Jethro first met, he said he wouldn't tackle the job without you. You told him that if so, he will never be able to take any credit for the corruption's collapse. He was okay with that, and with all this, none of it will be traceable back to him."

"I remember. Those words came out of my mouth without my planning to say them ahead of time, but I knew I was telling the truth. I also told him that another woman will be highlighted as the one at the end of all the corruption. I have no idea who that will be, James."

He nodded. "But God does."

"Yes, of course."

They snuggled together for almost an hour, each drinking a glass of wine while making small talk.

He kissed her on the cheek. "Let's go get some dinner. I'm ready for a steak. I'm thinking we can go to *333 Ocean Steakhouse.* What do you think?"

"That sounds great. I remember when we first went there with John and Kristal Silvers after church on Sunday. [Also seen in *God, Love and Stargazing* © 2020] That place has the best food we've ever had anywhere, and that's saying something."

The Sun was setting. In the evening traffic, it took them almost twenty minutes to get there, but they had to wait less than ten minutes to get a table. As usual their steaks were sizzling on metal platter when they were delivered to their table. James had a thick Porterhouse, and Deborah had a New York Strip.

As they ate, Deborah reviewed the first part of the confrontation schedule. "Each day's electronic deliveries will be at midnight Central Daylight Savings Time. We'll start with the Speaker, the Governor of his state, and two other governors. After that, deliveries will be every Monday, Wednesday, and Friday. The day before the first delivery, my blog will revolve around what the Bible says about wealth, sex, and power. After that, I expect my blog to reflect God's perspective on the confrontations and their reactions."

James chewed some steak and swallowed. "I think that the rest of the summer and on into the holidays, it's going to be a history-making time for our country." She nodded. He continued. "Next year is an election year, and it promises to be very interesting."

They lingered over dinner more than an hour and a half. After they finished dessert, they went home, shared a shower, went to bed, and turned off the lights.

As they were eating breakfast Saturday morning, Deborah's phone chirped. Seeing that it was Jethro, she pushed the speaker button. "Good morning, Jethro."

"Good morning Deborah. I know that you and James like to relax on Saturdays, so I won't keep you. It seems like starting Monday, our team should have daily teleconference calls to discuss our reviews of the files and directories. Both Fred and Saul have mentioned the possibility. What do you think?"

Deborah nodded as she looked at James and winked. He was smiling. "I think it's a good idea too, Jethro. Why don't you go ahead and automate the call to take place at 9:00 AM on Monday morning, okay?"

"Okay. You and James have a good weekend." He ended the call.

James spoke between bites. "We knew that this might happen."

"Of course."

"Yesterday I got a call from Jerry Rockwell, one of the elders at the church. Did you know that when he retired, he was a Fleet Admiral, which is a five-star rank?"

She shook her head. "I knew he retired as an officer in the Navy, but I didn't know his rank at retirement. What did he want?"

"He and almost a hundred of his old Navy friends got together four years ago and acquired an old nuclear submarine that had been mothballed. It has no weapons or advanced electronics, and for fun they've been turning it into what they think is a cruise ship for families and friends. It is no longer nuclear-powered, but the batteries are much larger, with enough storage for more than 24 hours of cruising. They charge it at the dock. If you and I want to join them on this cruise, we'll need to be in The Port of Cleveland before 11:00. There'll be snacks on board, but no meals available."

Deborah was grinning. "Absolutely! I wouldn't want us to miss an opportunity like this!"

It was late morning as they got under way, with one of the retired sub captains at the helm. The admiral and thirty-five guests met in a comfortable lounge most of which had previously been the mess hall. He spoke easily. "As I said earlier, this sub has been re-commissioned Nautilus, naming it after the sub in Jules Verne's novel, *20,000 Leagues Under the Sea*. Lake Erie is the shallowest of the Great Lakes. Although its maximum depth is over two hundred feet, it averages only a little over sixty feet. Since most of you are from my church, most of you know each other. We'll stay on the surface until we leave Erie and go into Huron. While we will submerge part of the time, we will probably spend most of our submerged time in Superior, because it is the deepest. Our plan is to be back here in Cleveland by seven o'clock, so dinner will be late for all of us. Below the water line we have installed several observation bubbles in the sides of this ship. They are not original equipment, of course. Since it's a beautiful and warm day, I suggest you spend time topside here on Erie, though you might get wet from the lake spray at times."

One of the crew members gave James and Deborah large towels as they went through a hatch onto the deck.

Deborah looked at her husband. "What do you say we relax and soak up some sun?"

"Good idea."

They might have fallen asleep except for spray from the bow. The sub was moving rapidly. When they stood up, they saw that they were going past Detroit. As they entered Huron, a Lieutenant told everyone on deck to go below because they could move faster under water. Brooke and James found comfortable seats by one of the bubbles and began using their phones to photograph some of the underwater life.

In church the following morning, James and Deborah enjoyed sharing their previous day's experiences with everyone before and after the worship service. Interestingly, the Bible lesson came from the last few chapters of the Book of Acts, when the Apostle Paul was under arrest and was sailing for Rome. Throughout the service, she found herself silently discussing the Apostle Paul' experiences with God and relating the Apostle's experiences with the things that had happened the day before. Several times she and James glanced at each other and knowingly nodded.

After the worship service, they sought out Jerry Rockwell. Deborah gave him a hug. "Good morning, Jerry. I want to thank you again for inviting us onto that cruise yesterday. We'll never forget the experience."

He nodded. "I'm glad you enjoyed yourselves. I've been meaning to ask you something, Deborah. When you led our Youth Fellowship meeting a month or so ago, I remember your saying that the corruption in the Washington Beltway was going to get cleaned up with God's help. Before I retired, I met with the Joint Chiefs of Staff on many occasions, attending luncheons with Washington's shakers and movers, and I've observed the corruption firsthand. Are you familiar with a video blog entitled *What Lies Ahead?*"

Deborah nodded. "Yes. I understand that the blogger is a woman who has quite a few subscribers." James squeezed her hand as she continued. "Why do you ask?"

"I subscribe to her blog. Since I hate all that corruption, I'm sending her a redacted copy of the last fifteen years of my military experiences' diary. I retired six years ago, but I'm hoping she will find it interesting or maybe useful. If you would like a copy of what I'm sending to the blogger, I can email it to you."

Deborah smiled broadly and nodded. "That would be great. After spending yesterday with you, I'm sure we'll enjoy reading about some of your experiences."

"Good. I'll send it as soon as my wife and I get home from church. Excuse me, but Becky is beaconing me." He walked off.

Softly, she told James, "This could be late-arriving gold!"

He nodded. "Yes. Will you forward it to Jethro?"

"Of course."

Later after lunch, when James was backing into their garage, Deborah's phone beeped. She saw that there was a large file attached from the Admiral. Once she and James were inside, she opened her laptop and sent the phone's signal to their great room's video screen. They both began reading.

"Now, that's interesting" was a phrase both used several times.

"Yes! I don't think he is on our list. Wow!" was another statement she made more than once.

"This will take us a while to read all this. I'll forward this file to Jethro right now." Her fingers flew rapidly over her keyboard for a moment, and then she went back to reading.

As the sun was getting low in the sky later that afternoon, her phone rang. "It's Jethro." She pressed her speaker button.

"Hey, Jethro, have you been reading this file from Admiral Rockwell?"

"Yes! Even heavily redacted, this journal is incredible. I'm going to ask Fred to have his crew work through this with him, and then Saul can add their results to the mix. This might add a day or two to our schedule, but who cares? How did you come by this, Deborah?"

"Yesterday, James and I were invited to join him on a cruise of the Great Lakes. This morning, after church, we thanked him for his letting us cruise with him, he reminded me of some of the things I've said about political corruption to our youth group. He asked me if I knew about my blog, not knowing I was the author, and then he told me he was sending it as a comment to the blog. He asked me if I would like a copy. I said yes."

"Deborah, have you scanned your blog's comments this afternoon?"

"Not yet. Why?"

"I scanned your blog's comments going back forty-eight hours. He didn't send this to your blog. He only sent it to you."

As Deborah's mouth dropped open, she looked at James, and he was staring at her wide-eyed. "Jethro, this must be his way of telling me that he knows that *What Lies Ahead* is my blog. The future implications of this are incredible, Jethro. I'm going to have to sit down with him soon for some dialog. Maybe James and I can play bridge with him and his wife one evening." She glanced at her husband, and he was nodding.

"That sounds like a good idea. The Admiral's journal puts a new spin on tomorrow morning's video conference."

Deborah sighed. "I agree. I'll see you tomorrow morning." They ended the call.

James was smiling. "I almost wish I didn't have to go to work tomorrow so I could spend the morning with you. I've got work waiting, though. Frank Schmitt flew into our Long Beach Airport last night and is staying at the Marriott on Airport Plaza. I'll be spending the next couple of days with him. There's a good chance he is going to accept our offer of a full professorship."

She nodded. "That's good." She closed her eyes for a moment, and then she opened them. "God has given me a little nudge. Tomorrow morning he's going to tell you something that will be important to both of us, though I don't know what it is. Why don't you have breakfast with him there at the hotel?"

James silently looked at her a moment. "You're serious?"

"Yes. We'll have a lot to talk about over dinner this evening – more than usual. What would you like me to fix for dinner? It's my turn."

He smiled. "We haven't had those sweet and zesty pork chops of yours for a while."

She nodded. "We'll have the sauce over rice and some plant-buttered spinach. Is Mr. Schmitt's wife with him?"

He also nodded. "Yes. I wanted her to have a chance to see the Long Beach area with him. Her name is Oma."

"That's an unusual name."

"I asked him about that. In Hebrew, the name means Cedar Tree."

Deborah was thoughtful. "I have a hunch that her relationship with Christ is deeper and stronger than her husband's. I don't know if that's important, but it could make for some interesting conversation. Let's invite them to join us for dinner. I'll fix some extra pork chops."

Chapter Five
Checking, Confirming, Proceeding

Oma was enthusiastic. "Deborah, these sweet and zesty chops are delicious."

"The sauce is mostly crushed pineapple and prepared mustard."

"They're wonderful! My grandparents wouldn't touch pork, but I'm glad I'm a completed Jew."

James smiled. "I gathered this morning at breakfast you're proud of your Jewish roots."

"Oh, definitely! Growing up, I loved my grandparents, and I have fond memories of sharing Jewish holiday meals with them."

Frank nodded. "Oma and I met just after she became a Messianic Jew. When I took her to the Lutheran church where my parents worshipped, she quizzed me and my family about our German roots and our take on the Holocaust. She had seen my Uncle Hans on television many times, and she had even more questions for him."

Deborah felt God's nudge deep within her and asked, "Who is your Uncle?"

Frank smiled. "He's my favorite Uncle, my Dad's older brother, Senator Hans Schmitt."

Deborah's eyebrows went up. "That Senator is your Uncle? He's one of the few good guys in Washington. He seems to be totally free of corruption."

Frank nodded. "That he is. He's part of a small network of Senators that work below the media's radar to battle corruption. His oldest daughter, my niece Maddy, is an often-sneaky insider that gathers information from Washington gossip that she filters for truth."

Oma was thoughtful, looking at Deborah. "I hope this.... Well, Frank and I are rather conservative. We have often posted tweets on Twitter with our views against the Washington establishment. James, are you familiar with a blog entitled *What Lies Ahead?*"

James was fascinated with what he was learning and nodded. "Actually, I'm quite familiar with it. On Twitter, I have recommended several of her blog posts to those who follow me. Why do you ask, Oma?"

"I like the blog because she is so often on target regarding what's going on in our governments, both national and state. I think she is an authentic prophet. Frank and I believe that much of our country's political corruption is going to collapse like a house of cards."

Frank nodded. "I'm not exactly looking forward to it because it is going to be painful for so many people. In Philadelphia, many of my students are troubled by what's going on with our government, while other students don't understand what's bothering them. When I'm counseling or in group discussions, I try to stay neutral and above the conflicting opinions, but it is often hard."

After dinner, the four of them played two rubbers of Bridge. In the first rubber, the cards seemed to favor James and Deborah, but Frank and Oma did even better during the second rubber. James took Frank and Oma back to their hotel while Deborah cleaned up after their little party.

James wasn't back yet when she phoned Jethro. "Do you remember my telling you that James was entertaining guests from Philadelphia this week regarding a future faculty position?"

"Sure. The musician's name is Frank Schmitt, right?"

"Right. He and his wife, whose name is Oma, were here for dinner with us, and we played a couple of rubbers of bridge. James is taking them back to the Long Beach Marriott."

"I've never understood why some people so passionately love play Bridge. I prefer computer games to card games."

"I understand, Jethro. That's not why I'm calling. James and I learned that Senator Hans Schmitt is Frank's Uncle, Frank's Dad's older brother. The Senator has a network below the media's radar with other Senators that are all fighting corruption."

"Wow. This has been totally under our radar as well."

Deborah was smiling, but it wasn't a video call, so Jethro could not see her. "Senator Schmitt' daughter, Frank's niece Maddy, is also important because she is a Washington insider who gets Washington gossip that she filters for truth using many of her many contacts. God is blessing us in unexpected ways!"

"Amen! Praise God! Six months ago, no one would have heard those words coming from my lips. God is definitely enhancing our efforts – first, the Admiral's journal, and now we're blessed with this." He paused, thinking. "Now, I pray that God will enhance my hacking skills."

"I'm sure those skills are some of the reasons God prompted me to get you to do this whole project."

"Right. I know. I'll silently make copies of the files in both Maddy Schmitt's computer and Senator Schmitt's network files. I won't get much sleep tonight, but with God's help, that'll be okay."

"What do you mean by 'silently'?"

"That means that when I used my God-given skills, no one knows I'm there or ever will know that I was there because know how to avoid leaving any kind of electronic trail behind me. I'll see you on the conference call tomorrow morning. Okay?"

"Okay, good night, Jethro." They ended the call.

Deborah heard the faint rumble of the garage door's opener. She got out two mugs and started making hot chocolate. James came in from the garage. "On the way home, they were very talkative. They say they're looking forward to my giving them a tour of the campus tomorrow. I didn't tell them why you and I are excited."

The microwave chimed, and Deborah took out the hot chocolate. "I called Jethro and summarized the evening for him. He says he'll probably be up all night, hacking into the Senator's network and his niece's computer." She handed James a mug. "I really like Oma and Frank. I hope things work out for them to move here."

"Me too. I have the URL for a video of this last Spring's Choral Concert that Frank conducted, which was shared with the Philadelphia Orchestra. It is absolutely thrilling."

"Okay, let's listen to it together the next time we take a Saturday vacation day and there's inclement weather."

The next morning's video conference started promptly, and Jethro led it off after their initial greetings. "You will notice that there is additional material this morning among our working directories and files. First, my program finished coordinating duplicate files in our project's entire server. That should simplify things for all of us."

Saul nodded. "I concur. That program evidently completed its work last Friday evening. I have already found it helpful."

"Good. The other program is still running, but it is providing us too much information to be effectively useful to us. We might have occasion to make use of those new files, but we have plenty of other new information that has come to us in the last forty-eight hours."

Fred was curious. "How so?"

"First, a retired Admiral provided Deborah with a redacted version of his journal, which covers more than thirty years. The older material is not going to be especially useful to us except as history, but much of the recent material provides verification that was sorely needed. Fred, have two or three of your people start working through that journal."

"Okay."

"The other new directory on our server is entitled *Clean Senators*. Saul, I'd like you to begin by reading through the files, put your keen intellect to work on it, and pray about what you read."

"Why is this so important?" Saul was shaking his head.

"It never occurred to us that there could be corruption-clear senators who were interested in doing exactly what we're doing. I've been up all night going through this, and these files provide us with some amazing new material. Also, Senator Hans Schmitt's daughter is an insider that has been brilliantly gleaning Washington gossip for the truth. Her intellect might be equal to yours, Saul."

"Indeed. If this work parallel's ours, we may gain some useful insights."

Deborah jumped in. "That's exactly right, Saul. I'm with Jethro in wanting you to dig into this. Today's new material means more work, but it will mean greater effectiveness in the end. By the way, this afternoon I am depositing additional funds into the accounts of all three of you. I deeply appreciate your efforts."

The video conference continued for more than an hour before they decided to meet at the same time the next day. When Deborah hung up, she got a secure text asking her to confirm the transfers of funds to Jethro, Saul, and Fred. She murmured, "All that God does, God does well" as she confirmed the transfers. She then went to the bedroom, knelt on the bed, and prayed.

She was still praying when her phone chirped just before noon. It was James, and she answered. "Hey handsome."

"Hey. Frank and Oma have asked if you can join us for lunch. How about it?"

"Where shall I meet you?"

"I'm thinking *The Breakfast Bar* on Atlantic Avenue. Okay?"

"Sure! I can eat breakfast at any time of the day. How soon?"

"Let's make it 12:30. Love you."

"I love you too." The call ended.

Deborah looked at her phone, thinking. Opening her contacts list, she scrolled down to the Admiral's number and touched it.

"Hello Deborah."

"Hello. First, this is a secure call, okay?"

"Okay. Let me go to another room." There was a pause. "Okay. Evidently, you've guessed that I know it's your blog."

"Right. Are you familiar with the name Jethro Underwood?"

"If it's the man I'm thinking of, he's the hacker that confronted more than a dozen government agencies to point out their security flaws. He then fixed them, right?"

"Right. Jethro is a friend who has secured both my phone and my computer."

Deborah heard him chuckle. "Deborah, if he's your security man, there's no one on Earth who is better than he is at what he does, and he does it with a sense of humor. The day he pointed out the Pentagon computer's flaws, those trying to call other agencies got a picture of the Kremlin, with two choices. One said, 'I don't care about my computer's security flaws. I want to continue to my destination.' The other one said, 'I want a free consultation with Jethro Underwood and have him fix my computer's security problems.' There was plenty of embarrassment to go around, all over the beltway."

"Admiral, I'm making this call because if you ever have reason to call me, whether about church business or any other business, you and I have this security."

"It occurs to me that this might be a subtle way of anticipating with me that I'll want to talk about one of your blog entries."

"That may well be true, Admiral, but I will never betray you."

"I believe you, and it is mutual."

"Thank you. I'm meeting my husband and some friends for lunch, so I must go. Bye"

"Bye, Deborah."

She parked near *The Breakfast Bar* with a few minutes to spare, but the others were already inside. As they ate Oma related to them how most of her family did not survive World War II. Frank's family was part of a resistance group that help support Dietrich Bonhoeffer and others in German concentration camps. The four of them were beginning to establish friendships.

That evening, Jethro put through a video call to Deborah. "Good evening, my friend. The new material we acquired is confirming and re-enforcing the material we had already prepared. I'm ready to proceed, aren't you?"

Deborah nodded. "I've been constantly praying. I agree. Do you still want to begin with the Speaker of the House and the three governors, sending the files from your hidden server?"

"Yes. At midnight Central Daylight Time Monday morning, the files will be delivered to forty-seven key media outlets and the politicos themselves. Wednesday night, it will be President Dough and three U.S. Senators, also as planned. I don't see any reason at this point to alter our planned schedule for the next month."

A sense of divine peace enveloped Deborah. She knew that God was at work within what they planned to do. "Go for it, Jethro, and let's keep our entire crew hidden, including ourselves. Right?"

"Exactly!" Jethro nodded. "When are you going to post to your blog again?"

"It'll be the first thing tomorrow morning. Let's talk about reactions tomorrow evening."

"Right." He ended the call.

James had been listening in on the other side of their great room. "Finally! Do you still think that all the confrontations will be delivered by mid-October?"

She smiled. "Yes, dear. I think you can go ahead with working out the details for our vacation in Lake Tahoe at the end of November. I'm probably as tired as you are. Let's worship and go to bed."

Chapter Six
Unexpected Tragedy

The next morning, James and Deborah watched a news capsule on a monitor in their bedroom while they got dressed.

> *...The emails were received at dozens of media outlets at 10:00 P.M. Pacific Daylight Time, which was 1:00 AM in our nation's capital. Everything in the files that were attached to the emails appeared to be authentic when first examined. Shockwaves are traveling through the news outlets and across the Internet....*

When the reports started to repeat, James switched it off. "We can watch updates later." He looked at his watch. "We're already later than usual. What can we fix for breakfast that's fast? Waffles and sausages?"

She nodded. "We got some boysenberry syrup a couple of days ago from our grocery shipment. We have plenty of juice in addition to coffee."

He shook his head. "I'd like Earl Grey this morning, for a change."

"Okay. I had another vivid dream last night. I remembered a Bible study of Acts 8 and Phillip the Evangelist's encounter with the Ethiopian Eunuch. If you see me disappear sometime today, don't worry."

"Really!"

She smiled. "I trust the Lord, and so do you."

It only took them a few minutes to get sausages and waffles ready in their air fryer. As they were drinking the last of their Earl Grey tea, Deborah said, "This boysenberry syrup was a nice change. I...." She disappeared as James stared in surprise.

Sighing, he got up and put their dishes in the dishwasher. Looking at his watch, he decided to skip brushing his teeth. He put on his green blazer that he had hung over a nearby chair, and he went out to the garage. As he drove down their driveway, the garage closed behind him. He headed down Hill Street. Halfway down the hill, the car exploded. The explosion was heard as far away as downtown Los Angeles and created a deep crater wider than the street.

At that moment, Deborah was sitting on the steps in front of the Lincoln Memorial in Washington, D.C. She was still in her same clothes, but she was wearing the Audrey Hepburn mask. She could feel it clinging to her face. Seeing the White House in the distance, she knew she should walk there. Suddenly, pain filled her. She knew something terrible had happened to James, but she didn't know what. She took out her phone to call him, but her call went straight to voice mail.

As she walked towards the White House, only a few people noticed she was there. At the security gate of the White House, she stopped. "Good morning. I am the woman who writes the blog known as *What Lies Ahead*. I'm here to see the President."

The guard nodded, picked up a phone, and relayed what she said. A few minutes later, he said. "President Dough will see you. Please proceed." He gestured towards the front doors.

As she continued to walk, she had an intimate sense of God's powerful presence and peace that subdued her concern for James. Inside, she was escorted to a small office, which she somehow knew was adjacent to the Oval Office. A man sitting at a desk in the little office stood up. "Good morning. The President will see you in just a moment. Deborah nodded and stood still. The man's phone buzzed. He listened, and then he went to a door and opened. "This way, please."

As she stepped inside, she recognized she was in the Oval Office, and the President was standing there to greet her. "Good morning. Please be seated." He gestured, and she sat down. "I must say, I am surprised by this visit. May I assume that your visit is related to the emails received by many news outlets last night?"

"If you wish, Mr. President, you may assume what you prefer. I have no objection."

The President half-smiled. "Then, instead of my making assumptions, why don't you tell me why you are here."

Deborah nodded, as suddenly she knew. "Mr. President, I personally did not send those emails. It is safe to say, however, that the Creator of the Universe has not been pleased with your behavior since you were sworn in as President or prior to that, swearing to do things you have failed to do faithfully."

"I assure you, that is not true."

"President Dough, you have a pleasant demeanor, but God is omniscient. While you might be able to fool me and countless other people, God knows the entire truth about every single person on Earth. He knows even our every thought."

The President stared at her for a moment. "Why are you telling me this?"

"During the coming weeks, the light of truth is going to be shining into the darkest corners of many lives associated with our national and state governments. God is mercifully and graciously allowing you a choice. You can either wait and see how virtually all your corrupt life will be truthfully exposed, or you can get a jump ahead of the news, repent, and become a servant who is faithful to both our country and to our God. The choice is yours."

As President Dough opened his mouth to respond, Deborah vanished from the oval office. He was stunned.

Deborah was instantly in a taxicab that was coming to a stop in Los Angeles at the entrance of KUBN, the network television center where Nicholas Terry worked. [Also seen in *A Marriage of Miracles* © 2020] She paid her driver and went inside. At the reception desk, the receptionist stared at her. "You're the woman who blogs *What Lies Ahead*." I watch it every day. May I help you?"

"Nicholas Terry is not expecting me, but I'd like to sit down and talk with him."

"Just a moment, I'll see if he's available."

Moments later, Nicholas Terry came to a nearby doorway. "Hello! I was just telling one of our producers that I wanted to interview you, and here you are. We have studio time available, but if you'd rather, we can talk in my office first."

Deborah shook her head. "Let's go to the studio." After they sat down, a microphone was clipped to her collar, and a makeup artist approached. She held up her hand and shook her head again. "The mask I'm wearing will have to do. Makeup will not be appropriate." The artist stopped and looked at her carefully. Deborah smiled. "Yes, it is a mask. It was made by an incredible artist in another country." The makeup artist turned and disappeared into the darkness behind the studio's lighting.

Nicholas took a deep breath and let it out. "Since you're wearing a mask, what shall I call you."

"If you wish, you can call me Deborah. She was a prophet in the book of Judges in the Old Testament."

"Okay. Let's begin." He paused. "At your request, I'll call you Deborah for the purposes of this interview. Today, the biggest thing in the news is the email that was delivered to hundreds of news outlets and to other people. Are you familiar with this story, and are you connected to it?"

"I am familiar with it. Several months ago, I said in my blog, quote:

> *Corruption in the Washington Beltway is going to end. God is at work. Some of the most corrupt individuals will move out of the beltway and fade into history's scrap heap. Some will repent and start to serve faithfully, getting them favorable reviews by future historians. Some will die.*

You can check your records. That is an exact quote. What I predicted is now beginning to take place."

"You say it is beginning to take place. Are you saying that there are more emails forthcoming?"

"As I have said many times in my blog, 'All that God does, God does well.' Over the coming weeks there will be many people who will be embarrassed, ashamed, or both. I have no doubt of that."

The interview continued for nearly a half-hour, but she gave away no secrets that she and Jethro shared. Afterward, Nicholas Terry wanted a phone number or email where she could be reached. She simply answered, "You can post a reaction to one of my blog posts, and I might respond."

After saying goodbye to Nicholas, she went down a small hallway to a restroom. With surprising ease, she splashed water on her face, slipped off her mask, and put it in her purse, where she also put the vest she had been wearing. In Washington, the weather had been cold. Now in Southern California, it was much warmer.

Outside the KUBN studios, Deborah got into another taxi. "Please take me to Signal Hill in Long Beach. I'll have you let me off at the monument at the top of the hill that marks the place where oil was discovered in the area."

"Yes, Ma'am."

The traffic was moderately heavy. As they went down the Long Beach Freeway, her mind was upon James, and she wondered what had happened to him. Suddenly, she had an idea, and she called her church. "Celia, this is Deborah. I've been cooped up at KUBN studios in Los Angeles. I've tried to reach James, but his phone goes directly to voicemail. Have you heard anything from him?"

"Oh Deborah! I've been praying for you! Early this morning, James was driving down Hill Street from your house, and his car exploded! The explosion could be heard for many miles and the crater that was formed made the street impassable to drive on!" Stunned, Deborah didn't say anything. "Deborah, are you there?"

"Yes, Celia, I'm here. I'll have my taxi take me there to the church. I need to pray. Can you stick around to take me home then? My car is at home."

"Sure! I'll be glad to. I'm so sorry, Deborah!"

"Thank you, Celia. I'll see you soon." She put her phone away and leaned forward to speak to her driver. "There's a change of destination, sir. My husband was in his car on Signal

Hill early this morning when it exploded. I need you to take me to my church. It's Ximeno Christian Church. It's on Cherry, just south of Anaheim. You can get off on Atlantic Avenue, go east to Cherry, and then turn south."

"Okay, Ma'am. I'm sorry your husband was in that car. A while ago, the Chief of Police in Long Beach said he thought that it might be the work of EX-20. Again, I'm sorry, Ma'am."

"Thank you."

When they got to the church, she paid the driver and went inside. She and Celia hugged, and then Deborah went into the sanctuary. She laid down on her face in the middle aisle and wept. She was not aware of Pastor Jerry coming in and sitting down at the rear as the sun was getting low in the sky.

Finally, Deborah got up and turned to go. She saw her pastor sitting there. "Good evening. How long have you been here?"

"It doesn't matter, Deborah." They hugged. "You probably don't feel like cooking. If you'd like to join us in the parsonage, we've plenty of food."

She shook her head. "Thank you, but I'm really not hungry. Even though I've spent the last few hours praying, there's calls I must make."

He nodded solemnly. "Okay. Call me if you need me."

They walked out together, and then Celia took her home. Going inside, she sat down in a recliner with her phone and called her parents, George and Alexandra. "Hi, Mom?"

"We know about what happened, Alexandra. We knew you'd call as soon as you could. We're so sorry."

Her dad confirmed. "Yes, Deborah. This must be horribly painful for you."

"It is. I've been in prayer most of the afternoon. The Evil One sometimes wins skirmishes, but he ultimately loses the war. I just am not ready to talk about it right now. Would you join me at my church this Sunday? Maybe I'll feel like visiting with you afterwards."

Her parents heard her silent signal that they knew so well. She wasn't ready to talk with them, and that was all they needed to know. "Okay, dear, we'll see you on Sunday. We love you."

"I love both of you, too." She ended the call and went to her speed-dial directory. She pushed a familiar button.

"Hey Deborah! The reactions are as we expected so far. What do you think?"

"Jethro, just after I left this morning, James was driving down Hill Street when his car exploded."

"Holy!... That was your James' car?"

"The Long Beach Police Chief says he thinks it is the work of EX-20. I hope there will be enough evidence for proof in a courtroom."

"Right. If any agency can sort this out, it's ATF."

"There's probably not enough left of James' body to warrant a casket. As I reminded my parents a few minutes ago, evil sometimes wins skirmishes, but the Devil ultimately losses the war." She paused. "I won't say much at tomorrow morning's video conference, so you'll have to carry the ball. Send me an email afterword if there's anything important to discuss."

"Okay. Again, I'm so sorry! I know how much you loved each other. I'll see you tomorrow."

"Okay." She hung up. She called the police department. James' body was obliterated instantly. It was an unusual bomb involving an unknown explosive coupled with thermite. ATF was in charge. There wouldn't be results of the testing for weeks.

Deborah slept only sporadically as she tossed and turned that night. While she was reading the Bible the next morning, her phone beeped a secured email.

> *Deborah. I'm taking your disaster personally. With whatever it takes, I will identify the killers. No charge. You've already paid me more than enough. Like I said, it's personal. Saul*

She knew that Saul had sources that were exclusive and far-reaching. If he could arrange it, the bomb makers were doomed.

For breakfast, Deborah managed to consume a good-sized bowl of congee with bacon.

During the video conference call, she tried to focus upon what was going on, but it was hard. Her grief fogged her thinking. After the video call, she prayed through the disaster with The Lord.

The next batch of files were attached to media sent via emails, as scheduled. The internet lit up when word got out that some of the media that received emails were in Europe, Latin, and Asia. There had been one suicide almost immediately, and one senator had resigned with expressions of shame. The confrontations seemed to be beginning to gain a foothold on the Internet.

After she had prayed for over an hour after the conference call, Deborah took out her phone and called her pastor. "Pastor Jerry, since James' body was obliterated, can we set aside a memorial time during Sunday's worship?"

"Sure. We'll also set up a reception area for after worship, where people can share memories and look at pictures of him. During worship, we can also have him on the video screen."

"Okay. I'll email some pictures and videos to Celia."

"Good. How are you holding up?"

"I'm not sure, but I'll get through this."

"I know. I'm still available when you need me."

"I know. Bye, Pastor Jerry." She hung up.

Opening her laptop, she spent several hours replaying memories that had been record during her marriage of nearly seven years to James. She zipped a few dozen pictures and a few videos together and sent them to Celia.

At the beginning of each of the Mondays, Wednesdays, and Fridays that followed, batches of emails were sent with attached files. Friday night's batch was focused upon President Dough, along with the Governors of four states. Sunday morning, the President announced that he would hold a press conference that evening.

At the reception after Sunday's worship service, George and Alexandra, her parents, stood with her as she was talking to people who were expressing their condolences. Suddenly, across the hall, she recognized someone she hadn't seen since high school. She smiled and waved.

He walked towards her and hugged her. "Deborah! It is so good to see you! I'm so sorry about James. He was a truly a great guy. I'm sure Jesus' welcomed him home with open arms!"

"David!! It never occurred to me that I would see you here today." She turned. "Do you remember my parents? This is my Mom and Dad, David." They greeted each other.

"David, we graduated from Wilson a long time ago. I thought that you and Linda were living in Kansas City!"

He shook his head. "Linda died of breast cancer two years ago. Afterward, I was aimlessly kicking around for a while, but most of our friends and family are still here in Long Beach, so last month I moved back here and into an apartment on Livingston Drive in Belmont Shore. How are you holding up?"

"I'm putting one foot in front of the other."

David nodded. "When Pastor Jerry talked about recent events, I was reminded of something interesting that was covered on UBN. The White House visitor logs show that the blogger of *What Lies Ahead* visited with President Dough on the same day as the explosion. Nicholas Terry says that can't be true because the blogger was in Los Angeles doing an interview with him at the time the visitor log says she was with the President. Somebody doctored the visitor log. I would imagine only the President has that authority. He's announced a press conference for this evening."

Deborah nodded. "I'll think about that after I get out of this fog of grief. When this reception winds down, do you want to get some lunch and share some memories?"

David smiled. "That sounds good."

That afternoon, Deborah and David spent a couple of hours munching on tacos, sharing memories, and offering one another mutual comfort for the deaths of their spouses. It occurred briefly to Deborah that maybe romance for them might be kindled later.

In the evening, President Dough's press conference lit up the Internet again. He made several shocking statements.

- *"I did not know when last night's files would become public, but I was expecting them."*
- *"I am profoundly ashamed and embarrassed by what everyone must now know."*
- *"I will not seek re-election at the end of this term."*
- *"I'm going to do my best to undo as much damage I have done as possible."*
- *"When congressional committees investigate me, I will answer all questions truthfully and fully. Others may well be embarrassed or ashamed by my truthful answers."*

The press conference lasted more than an hour, as the President answered numerous questions. As Deborah listened, she recognized how gracious and merciful God was towards President Dough. Her appearance at the White House and her being recorded in the visitor logs was never mentioned during the press conference, and it became only a footnote for future historians.

When the press conference was over, she turned off her video display and took out her phone. She felt the need to call Saul and thank him for his text.

"Deborah. It is good to hear from you. How are you doing?"

"I'm holding on. I'm calling to thank you for your text. Earlier today someone told me that if any agency can get to the source of the explosion, that it was ATF."

"It may happen that way, but my investigation is not following the chemical trail or the trails of other evidence on the scene. I have been in my business for many years, and I have many friends on both sides of the law. I have called in some favors, and I will possibly call in more. I watched the President's press conference. I was impressed with his repentance. Were you?"

"I was. The weeks ahead will either confirm it or negate it."

"True. I saw the interview that you did with Nicholas Terry. He has since said that the White House visitor logs show you there in Washington at almost the same time as he interviewed you. What do you say?"

"That's very diplomatic of you, Saul. You're a loyal friend. Are you familiar with someone in the New Testament named Phillip or as Phillip the Evangelist?"

"Certainly. His encounter with the Ethiopian Eunuch comes to mind."

"After Phillip baptized the Eunuch, Phillip disappeared and reappeared somewhere else. The morning of the explosion, I disappeared from in front of my beloved James and found myself sitting on the steps in front of the Lincoln Memorial in Washington. I walked to the White House, and the rest you know."

"I remember hearing both you and James saying, 'All that God does, God does well.' Indeed!"

Chapter Seven
Graciously Sustained

When James' parents were killed by a terrorist bomb, Deborah had said to him,

> *Grief never ends but does change. It is simply a passage and not a place to stay permanently. It is not a sign of weakness or a lack of faith. It's the price of love.*

Now, that same advice was being fulfilled in herself. Whenever she focused upon what God had given to her and to Jethro to be accomplished, she was able temporarily to put her grief aside. She saved her tears for her alone time in her big house on Signal Hill. When she couldn't eat at all for several days, she had a hunch, went to a drugstore, and tested herself. She was pregnant. Seeing the result, her first thought was *James must be smiling in heaven.*

After her doctor confirmed that she was about two months along, she told Pastor Jerry. He smiled. "You must be thrilled!"

Deborah nodded. "My life is going to be fuller from now on." They spent some time that morning talking about potential implications, both legally and financially because of her wealth. She knew when she left Pastor Jerry's office, she had hard work to do ahead.

Late in the evening the following day, Jethro called her. "Good evening, my friend. How are you doing?"

"I'm coping a little better. What's new?"

"I've been thinking about your interview with Nicholas Terry. What was your impression of him? You seemed very relaxed with him."

Deborah was thoughtful. "That's true," she said confidently. "In person, he's a very likable guy as well as brilliant. He's almost totally transparent. In addition to being honest, he didn't interview me with any agenda beyond basic curiosity. Politically, he seems non-partisan, though he didn't say so. Why do you ask?"

"I had my lawyer order me a mask from that artist that made yours, and it came this morning. I have decided I'm going to let Nicholas Terry interview me as 'Hacker Dude.'"

"Really! Who are you going to look like?"

"John Wayne. The mask came with a brown wig."

Deborah whooped. "That's fantastic! John Wayne's the perfect hero persona for you! When are you going to do the interview?"

"There's a UBN station in Cincinnati, and he's going to be there over the next few days because of the student demonstrations there. I'm going to wander among the students as John Wayne, and I'll try to get Nicholas Terry's attention."

"Great! I'll support you with prayer. Call me after your interview."

"Okay." He ended the call.

Mid-afternoon, the next day, "John Wayne" entered the UBN station in Cincinnati as arranged. As Jethro walked into a lounge to wait until his interview's scheduled time, he looked across the room, and his legs turned to rubber. His heart began pounding. He had seen the woman's pictures and videos countless times, but this was different. It was Alice Schiffer, who had been born in Berlin in Germany on the same day he had been born in Long Beach California.

Jethro reached deep within himself and recovered his composure. "Good afternoon. Aren't you miss Alice Schiffer?" He tried to use a western drawl.

She laughed. "That's not a bad impression of John Wayne! Yes, I am! May I ask who's behind the mask?"

"For Nicholas Terry, I'm 'Hacker Dude.' I'm somewhat involved in the emails that are confronting politicians."

"Excellent!"

Nicholas Terry appeared in a doorway. "Miss Schiffer? I'm ready for you."

"Okay. Just a moment." She turned to Jethro. "John, let me put my number into your phone."

He didn't hesitate. "Okay." He handed it to her.

She entered her data and pressed send. Her phone rang in her purse. She handed his phone back to him and took out hers. She answered it, hung up, and identified the number as John Wayne. "Okay. John, call me sometime next week. Let's talk."

"Okay." His heart was still pounding.

Alice followed Nicholas into the studio. Jethro looked at his watch. He was scheduled for fifteen minutes later, but he knew that it might be longer. It was.

When Jethro went in as Alice left, he was relaxed, and Nicholas undoubtedly sensed it. "My next guest may look like John Wayne or one of his descendants, he identifies himself simply as 'Hacker Dude.' So, you make you're living as a hacker?"

Under the mask, Jethro had a small device cemented onto his Adam's apple that altered his voice slightly. "I do quite a bit of hacking, but it is not my only source of income. There are parts of the Internet that provide excellent income if you know where those locations are and have the skills to satisfy the interests of clients. There are many politicians in the news in recent days that are very sloppy with their internet skills. I won't work for them, however, because of their ethics."

"If you won't work for them, do you work against them?"

It was the question that he wanted Nicholas to ask. "I've had opportunities to do so, and it has been both profitable and pleasurable."

The interview continued for the better part of an hour. When it was over, Alice had left, but Jethro had expected that.

At that moment in Port St. Lucie, Florida, Fred Drake was working with some of his operatives, assembling files for future confrontation emails. When his front door opened, Fred looked up and saw a half dozen armed people. "Which one of you is Fred Drake?" Fred stood up. "You're the one we want. The rest of you...."

The man's voice trailed off. He and the others who came in put their weapons on the floor and raised their hands. Fred and his operatives looked towards the rear, where a squad of fully armed U.S. Marines had silently entered from the rear. A man that Fred recognized a Marine captain was also a friend from his church. "Mr. Drake, you and the others can get back to work. We'll take care of this little interruption." He gestured to one of his lieutenants.

As the other Marines put the interlopers into a military truck that had pulled up and was waiting in the street, the captain looked at Fred.

Fred shook his hand. "You showed up in the nick of time, Paul. Did you just happen to see the others come in?"

The captain shook his head. "You have spoken out against corruption in Washington at church. Some of my friends and I have been keeping an eye on your business when we're not on duty. A few weeks ago, when the first emails were delivered to media outlets, I told one of my superiors about you. He cut orders to keep a rotation of men on duty just in case." He paused and smiled. "We've got your back, Fred." They shook hands.

Fred's operatives in his office applauded. One of them said, "Hoo-rah!"

Paul grinned, waved, and went on out to the truck.

Fred looked around. "Okay, that's an unexpected blessing. Let's get back to work." He would report it the next morning at the video conference. He took out his phone to call Deborah.

Meanwhile, in Los Angeles Jethro went to his SUV that was parked in a multi-level parking garage where he had parked. His windows were tinted, so no one could see inside as he took a washcloth, soaked it with bottled water, and pressed it to his face. The mask came off easily, and he put the voice-altering disk in the same case as the mask.

The traffic was heavy as he set out for home. He pressed a button on his steering wheel. "Call Deborah's cell phone."

"Hey, Jethro, how did your interview with Nicholas go?"

"It went as expected. I was able to insert cues into my answers to lead him into questions I wanted him to ask. Nicholas is a good man. When I get home, I'll watch it and evaluate both of us. It's part of being somewhat of a control freak."

"I'll look for it. I watch most of his interviews. As I said before, he seems highly intelligent."

"He is that." Jethro paused. "Before my interview, I got to chat briefly with Alice Schiffer. She was interviewed before me."

"Really! I've seen a couple of her movies. What did you think of her?"

Jethro paused. "To say I was impressed would be a massive understatement, my friend. She gave me her cell number and asked me to call her next week. Just telling you about her makes my heart pound. No one else in my whole life has ever had that kind of effect upon me."

"So, you're smitten, as my parents sometimes say?"

"Is that what I am? If so, I know I've never been smitten before."

"I've got some news for you that you might find interesting?"

The traffic had halted for Jethro. "What's that?"

"I got a call a few minutes ago. Fred and a half-dozen of his operatives were working in his office when some armed men and women came in. They asked for Fred, and when he stood up, out of nowhere a squad of Marines appeared and took the others into custody. Evidently, they took their prisoners back to the Marine Corps Training Center, which is their base. Fred says he'll give more details during tomorrow morning's video conference if our team wants to know more. I certainly do."

The traffic started moving again. "I do too. I was surprised when we got support from Admiral Rockwell. I didn't anticipate having Marines backing us up on this either, did you?"

"No. God did not give me even a glimmer of this when I've been praying. This is interesting. Tell me more about meeting Alice Schiffer."

"It is a little embarrassing to tell you, but I had seen her pictures and a couple of movies, but this was different. My legs were shaking, and my heart was pounding."

"Well, if you two start dating, bring her up to my house for dinner. I've got great views in two directions."

Jethro laughed. "If that happens, it will be a genuinely great blessing, Deborah. I'm getting close to my turn off. We'll see each other tomorrow morning. Bye"

"Bye, Jethro." She closed her eyes for a moment. "Yes, Lord," she mumbled. Going down the hall, she pulled the hidden latch in the bookcase, and it pivoted to reveal the chute into the panic room. She jumped, and the bookcase pivoted back to its normal appearance behind her. At the bottom of the chute, she landed on the pad, and then she watched video monitors as she had with James previously. At first, she didn't see anything.

A green LED light indicated that the security company had not detected a problem. The stairs door into the attic in the ceiling of the laundry room seemed to be slowly moving downward. Deborah pressed a red button next to the green LED, and it immediately changed to red. The monitors were all touchscreen equipped, so she tapped that attic door twice, telling those monitoring the house what was happening.

Several minutes later, her phone chirped. She looked at the screen before answering. "Yes?"

"Everything's clear, Mrs. Maffett. Two men who had gotten into your attic are in custody and are on their way to the police station. They had no identification on them, and they have not said a word. Do you want a detailed report now, or do you want to be given a review tomorrow morning?"

Deborah sighed. "Tomorrow morning will be fine. I'd like level one monitoring until we talk tomorrow morning."

"Yes, ma'am. Sleep well."

"I'll try. Goodnight." She went straight to her bedroom. She looked up at the ceiling. "In Jesus name, I ask that all evil be driven from this house, and that the Holy Spirit fill this place according to Your will, Heavenly Father. Amen." After taking a shower, she went to bed. Turning off the light, she slept soundly for a full night's rest for the first night since James had died.

The next morning, in Mentor, Ohio, Saul Wolfe sat outside near Lake Erie, watching the sunrise. He had been sipping coffee from an insulated cup and praying for more than an hour. One of his neighbors jogged past him, and she waved. "Good morning, Jess." He said as he was waving back. He smiled and remembered when she had arrived a couple of months earlier and moved into a house a little further west.

The sun was just beginning to rise as his neighbor was jogging past him, going the other direction, when suddenly she dropped to one knee with a gun in her hand. She fired what he thought was three shots over Saul's head. He was stunned, his eyes wide, as she walked towards and past him, her gun still drawn. Saul turned, watching, with his mouth agape.

Pointing her gun at a body not ten feet from Saul, she nudged the body with her foot, and then she went further towards Saul's house to check on another body lying not a dozen feet from Saul's back door. He stood up. "What in the...." He was dumbfounded.

She nodded at him. "General Plummer has rented the house I'm in with four others. When the controversial emails began, the General decided to keep an eye on you as a measure of security for a man whose friendship he values highly. As I told you previously, my name is Jess. What I didn't tell you is that I'm in the Naval Reserves, and I used to be in the special forces command. For me, this morning was almost fun, though I'm sure you see it differently."

Wolfe almost grinned. "Thank you! Should I shake your hand, or can I give you a hug?"

She returned his grin. "A hug would be nice!"

He hugged her. "Thank you!"

"Thank you, too! My partner has already called for cleanup. They'll get here before the police can. I put two bullets in the one closest to you, and Jeff, my partner, got the other guy.

Wolfe turned around and walked towards the body of the one that was a dozen feet from where Saul's mug was still sitting on the beach. The man appeared to be Hispanic. Blood was oozing from the center of his chest and from just above the man's nose. Jess was obviously well trained and a crack shot. Saul sighed.

Jess came and stood beside him again. "The General will find out where these two came from and who hired them. He's already investigating alongside of ATF the death of your friend's husband on Signal Hill a few weeks ago. You know the General."

Saul nodded. Chris Plummer was the best at this kind of thing. Saul was glad that the General still had his back after all these years. He and Chris became friends when Saul worked with him in Viet Nam.

Saul looked at his wristwatch. He wanted to get some breakfast before the video phone conference with Deborah and the others. He looked at Jess. "I've got work to do, and I'm hungry." He saw some green military vehicles pulling up in front of his house. "Jess, when you're done here, I'll be glad to fix you some breakfast."

She smiled. "No thanks, Mr. Wolfe. I ate before I went on duty."

"Okay, maybe another time. Thanks again." He picked up his coffee mug.

"You're welcome."

Saul went into his house. General Plummer's crew had the two bodies off the beach quickly, so when the police arrived, they were simply told that Wolfe had been the host for some training in dealing with the public. When a Mentor Police lieutenant came to the door, Saul confirmed what the lieutenant had been told. Then he went back inside to eat his breakfast.

Saul led off the video conference by reporting what had happened earlier on his beach. He told his story precisely, somewhat like dictating to a secretary. At the end he said, "Chris Plummer and I have been good friends for most of my life. In Viet Nam, he was a newly commissioned captain when I was a grunt."

Jethro was curious. "Deborah, is it possible that your Admiral Rockwell is somehow involved in any of this?"

She smiled. "I'll have to ask him, but it's possible that the General and the Admiral were on the Joint Chiefs together at one time."

Jethro nodded. "I'll check on the *Political Nightmares* web site. There may well be some video of the two of them at some public functions. Deborah, you made an offer to me about dinner with Alice and me at your house. Let's talk more about that after this call is over."

"Okay. I have a suggestion for the group. It's just something for us to consider, and it just occurred to me yesterday. There's internet chatter about who is going to run for President starting next year. We will be done with our scheduled email confrontations early next month. I'd like all you to think about the possibility of our putting together email packages on the candidates who will be on the ballots the following year. If you want to do it, I will pay for all expenses. Just think about it for now."

The video call went on for another half hour, and then they signed off for the day. A few minutes later, Deborah was sipping a cup of hot chocolate when Jethro called again. "Hey, Deborah. Have you got a minute?"

"Sure. The invitation is still open."

"Good. Last evening, Alice and I were eating dinner at *333 Ocean Steakhouse*. I remember you told me once that you and James liked to eat there."

"We sure did. I think it's one of the best places to eat steaks in all Southern California."

"I now agree. Anyway, I told Alice that the blogger of *What Lies Ahead* has invited us to dinner, and she has wanted to meet you for a long time anyway."

Deborah knew something more than Jethro did about Alice. "This is excellent, Jethro. If Alice's schedule is open this weekend, why don't you and Alice come up to my house on Friday at 5:00?"

"That'll be great!"

She didn't tell Jethro that God had prepared Alice and Jethro for each other, and that they had been set up, brought together, and given to each other. The rest was up to them. Meanwhile, Deborah needed to prepare with prayer and plan the evening for them.

A few minutes later, her phone chimed an incoming call. She looked at the display. It was for West Coast Christian College Administration. "Hello, Mrs. Maffett?"

"Yes."

"Chancellor Wheeler here at West Coast Christian College would like to speak with you. Will you accept his call?"

She nodded absent-mindedly. "Of course."

A man's voice said, "Mrs. Maffett, this is Chancellor Wheeler. We have not talked since your husband was killed. How are you doing?"

"I'm getting by. Grief is passage that is part of life. What can I do for you, sir?"

"First, I want to share with you that your late husband's search for our Professor of Choral Studies resulted in our hiring a very capable man. I wish your husband could still here to see how well Frank Schmitt is fitting in. His wife, Oma, wants to continue her friendship with you but does not know how to reach you. May I give her your phone number?"

Deborah sighed. "You could, but if you give me her number, I will call her."

"Okay, I'll have my secretary text you with her number. The other thing I have called about today is the fact that your late husband's contract with us includes both a pension and an accidental death insurance policy, with you as the beneficiary."

Again, Deborah sighed. "Chancellor, I appreciate your telling me this, but I don't want the money. My lawyers here in Long Beach are Houser and Beam. I'll have them draw up paperwork for me to have James' widow's benefits rolled over into the Pension Fund of the college, and I'll donate the payout from the insurance into the Pension Fund as well. Also, when James' parents were killed, he inherited are portfolio of investments. I'm sure James would be pleased if I donate a portion to the college's endowment."

"That will be wonderful, Mrs. Maffett. On behalf of West Coast Christian College, thank you very much."

Chapter Eight
Cementing Relationships

Jethro and Alice pulled into Deborah's driveway in his Lexus at a few minutes before 5:00 on Friday evening. As he held Alice's door, she looked around in all directions. "The view from up here is wonderful." She pointed. "We can see a little of Catalina above the smog from here." Jethro took her hand, and they walked onto Deborah's porch and rang the doorbell.

Deborah answered the door only a moment after they rang her doorbell. "Good evening, Jethro! It's nice to meet you, Alice!"

"Good evening, Mrs. Maffett! I recognize you! "Aren't you the harpist in *New Rocks*? I've downloaded all your group's videos! I love your music!"

"Thank you! Come in! You can leave your coats here in the mud room if you wish. Then, come with me into the great room. Let's get comfortable." She led them to the conversation pit near the fireplace. "I have stuffed Cornish hens in the oven, but they won't be ready for a while." They sat down.

Jethro held Alice's hand when they sat down in a love seat. "I don't think I've ever thought about your music work. Have you and your group recorded anything recently?"

Deborah nodded. "The first time that *New Rocks* ever did a paid performance was when we were all students at Cal-State Long Beach, and we performed at the Long Beach Petroleum Club. Since then, we've performed there several times. The first weekend of this past November we played for a dance there, and it was recorded. It's being edited and should be posted online in a week or so." She paused. "I think I caught a glimpse of you two at Ximeno Christian Church last Sunday."

Jethro nodded. "Yes. After worship, Alice wanted to talk to Pastor Jerry."

She smiled. "My family in Germany is all Lutheran, so I was baptized as an infant. I told Pastor Jerry I wanted to follow

Jesus' example, and I'm going to spend some time with Pastor Jerry to make sure my heart is in the right place."

"Good! Will that be hard to fit into your schedule?"

"I'll make it fit. Right now, I'm shooting a pilot for a Sam Winter TV production. If the pilot is picked up, I'll be in a weekly video series. Sam is a Christian, and most of the cast and crew are Christian, so it will be easy to get time set aside for worship."

Deborah nodded. "Are you and Jethro praying with and for each other?"

Alice seemed puzzled. "With and for?"

"Yes. It's important. One of the qualities of our triune God that is often mentioned is that our heavenly Father is eternal, which is connected to God being omnipresent."

Jethro grinned. "The first time I ever heard that word was when you and I first met for breakfast on the Queen Mary. When I got home that night, I went to an online unabridged dictionary and looked it up. I think of myself as smarter than average, but just like God's being eternal, it is hard for me to wrap my mind around all the qualities of God."

Deborah smiled. "Professional theologians enjoy talking about the qualities of God, but you're like most people, and discussing spiritual things in temporal words can be a real challenge. In this corner of the house, the great room faces both east and south. I sometimes sit here for the sunrise after I worship, but before I fix breakfast." She pointed. "That's Santa Catalina Island over there, peaking above the smog at sea level."

Alice nodded. "I mentioned that to Jethro when I got out of the car. The smog must not be very deep today."

Deborah shook her head. "I've not seen any weather reports today, but that is probably more fog than smog we're seeing from up here. Many years ago, there was a restaurant up here called The Hilltop. My parents have told me that what is seen from up here blanketing what's below us is typically fog. When they were dating and ate at The Hilltop as teens, smog pollution wasn't a real problem then."

"Do your parents still live in this area?"

"Yes. They live over there in the Los Altos area." Deborah pointed. "Catalina was infested with rattlesnakes when people first settled there. The Wrigley family, whose big business was chewing gum, bought the island at the beginning of the twentieth century. They brought in wild boar from Australia to kill the snakes, but it was nearly a hundred years before the ecological balance was restored on the island. Right after the snakes were eradicated, for instance, the island's jackrabbit population exploded with snakes not there to feed on them."

Alice smiled. "Jethro and I were over there, last weekend at Avalon. It's a beautiful little town."

"Yes. My late husband, James, and I went there several times. He was in the car that exploded on Hill Street. Let's not talk about that right now."

Her guests nodded solemnly. "Anyway, God created all matter, energy, space, and time. That's basic for Christianity. Science is interested in the 'what,' 'when,' 'where,' and 'how' our universe was created. The Bible, in contrast, focuses primarily upon 'who' and 'why.'"

Again, Deborah pointed. "Let your eyes rest on the hilltop of Catalina, and think about how God is there, here, and everywhere." She paused. "Now, since God created time and isn't within its constraints, God is there, here, and everywhere at every moment of time."

The sky was slightly pink from the western sun as Deborah prayed. "Heavenly Father, in Jesus' name I ask that you let Alice and Jethro be present to Your divine presence and grant them a glimpse of your glory. Amen."

Alice and Jethro both sighed, and then they hugged. "I love you, Alice."

"I love you too."

He looked at her. "Did we just admit that we love each other?"

Tears were running down Alice's cheeks as she vigorously nodded.

Deborah watched silently for a couple of minutes. "This began when you asked me, Alice, about praying with and for each other." Both were looking at Deborah steadily. "Now, take each other's hands and close your eyes." They did. "Now that you understand what it means to be present to God's presence, you can be present to God's presence together, and you can present one another to God." She paused. "Ask God for whatever comes to mind, and then let the Holy Spirit flow over and through you, healing and redeeming you, as you are totally one in God's spirit as brother and sister in Christ."

Jethro quietly said. "Amen."

Alice said, "Amen. Something has changed, at least within me. Has something changed within you?"

He nodded. "Yes, but I don't have a clue as to what all has changed."

Deborah smiled. "You don't have to be in a hurry. God's timing is always perfect, so just let life flow. I don't know about you two, but I'm hungry. We can at least have our salads. The stuffed game hens are probably almost done." They were.

Later, when they had finished their desserts, they were having coffee and again sitting near the fireplace. "Alice, for the last several months I've been watching how God has been using Jethro on the sidelines of the political confrontations taking place in both our federal government and many of the state governments."

Alice nodded. "I've been both excited and relieved. As I have watched your blogs, I have known that God is at work in this cleanup of political corruption. I'm glad that you and Jethro can be part of what God is doing."

Deborah smiled. "I don't know what Jethro has revealed to you, and that's not really important as far as I'm concerned."

"Really? Why?"

"I have prayed that God grant you the vision to see God's will clearly, Alice. I've also asked God to steadily increase and grow your faith, so that you can believe in whatever God reveals to you. Even more importantly, God is giving you the courage to trust God with every aspect of your life."

Alice's mouth hung open slightly as she stared at her. "Forgive me, but I have to ask again. Why?"

Deborah was thoughtful. "Just as God is continuing to use Jethro and his skills, and just as surely as God has been speaking through me, the time is coming soon when God is going to begin speaking through you as well. Don't try to make it happen. Just live a humbly prayerful life."

Alice nodded. "Somehow I know that tonight you and I have begun a wondrous friendship."

"Yes."

After the worship service on the following Sunday, Deborah and Admiral Rockwell chatted privately. "Yes, I've known General Plummer for many years. We talk two or three times a week. Our wives get together to shop or have lunch regularly. He's slightly younger than I am, so he's still on active duty while I'm retired. He and your friend, Saul, are friends, and General Plummer has better investigative instincts than me, but I did many favors for him before I retired."

Deborah nodded. "I think the General is working with Saul as we speak."

"Yes. When we were both serving on the Joint Chiefs, he once told me that Saul can work miracles and is probably the best investigator that's ever lived. That's saying something."

She smiled. "Definitely. His fees are high, but he earns them."

The admiral laughed. "The General told me also that when Saul decides to do a favor for a friend, that he's like a bulldog that won't let go until he's finished with what he sets out to do."

Inside, Deborah felt relieved. "Thank you. This is good for me to hear." She smiled genuinely.

"I think you and I are on the same page." He looked over her shoulder. "Oops! Becky is gesturing at me. Duty calls. I'll see you next Sunday."

"Have a good week, Admiral."

He quickly joined his wife, and they went out towards the parking lot. Alice and Jethro approached Deborah as the Admiral was leaving. Alice hugged Deborah. "Tomorrow morning, I'm scheduled for a mammogram because of a lump I discovered last week. When I was taking a shower this morning, the lump was no longer there. Is it possible that God healed me when Jethro and I prayed with and for each other the first time the other night?"

Deborah nodded. "It's possible, although God has not revealed that to me in a specific way. Call me when you have the result." She turned to Alice's future husband, though they didn't know it yet. "Have you secured her phone for conversations with me?"

Jethro nodded. "I did as soon as I got home Friday night – or should I say, Saturday morning."

Deborah nodded again. "Make sure you two approach everything in terms of doing things God's way, on His terms, and for His glory."

"Absolutely!"

Monday morning, after Deborah, Jethro, Saul, and Fred finished their routine video conference, Saul had a call from General Plummer. "Good morning, General. Yesterday afternoon, Jess told me that I would probably hear from you today."

"Jess is reliable. I've gotten confirmation as to the individual who planted the bomb in James Maffett's car." He paused. "Most bombers have a so-called signature in terms of the materials and technology used. This guy is wanted in seven countries, and he's killed hundreds of people. Up until now, nobody has known his identity. He lives in Atlanta. We know it without any doubt, but you and I both know we can't put the bastard in jail."

"Thank you, General. I know what that means." The next morning, Saul invited Jess to join him for breakfast. As they were eating, he said, "I understand you once took out a drug boss at more than 1300 yards when you were in Special Forces Command."

Jess sipped her coffee. "General Plummer told me what he told you, I guess. I know who put the crater on the east side of Signal Hill in Long Beach, killing the husband of a special friend of yours, but the killer will never go to trial. I'll be on high alert with you for the next few months."

Saul nodded. "Couldn't a sniper just take him out?"

"Yes, but neither local police nor the FBI likes dealing with incidents like that. The media can be tenacious with their investigations, according to the General. This killer will be dealt with in a more specialized way because he's responsible for so many deaths."

"May I ask how?"

"I can't be sure, but dragon's breath is one option. It is not military ammunition. It is specialized and expensive ammunition that is usually used for celebrations like the Fourth of July. It's not even available in all states."

"Dragon's breath?"

"Yes. The shells are typically 12-guage in size, but the load is not buck shot or rock salt. It's phosphorus. When the shells are fired, there's a flame up to thirty meters long."

Saul half smiled. "It's not used by the military?"

"No. It has extremely limited range and accuracy, and at close range it can be dangerous to the user unless used very carefully. It's also hard on most 12-guage weapons. I once used a starter pistol to fire one in the air at a party. It's hard to scare me, Saul, but that shell did."

That evening, Saul subscribed to the daily news of a TV station in Atlanta. He also told Jethro about his conversations with General Plummer and with Jess.

Jethro was intrigued. "Do you find Jess attractive, Saul?"

"Certainly, I'm attracted to her, but she's less than half my age, and I'm a confirmed bachelor. I'll never get married." The question made Saul think, however. Then he did his best to put the thought of romance with Jess behind him.

Jethro didn't however, because he was in love with Alice. She was at his house when he told her, "Saul says he's attracted to Jess, but since she's less than half his age and he's a confirmed bachelor, they'll never have romance."

Alice was amused. "I'd dated a lot of guys before we met, so that first time we had lunch, I wasn't expecting anything. On a first date, I often did not kiss the guy good-bye, and if I did, I would kiss him on the cheek. For some reason, I decided to give you a quick con-committal kiss on the lips. When we did, however, my heart melted, my love."

He nodded. "I had seen pictures and videos of you before we met in the green room at KUBN, but when I walked in, my legs turned into rubber, and my heart started pounding. When you gave me your number and told me to call you, my life changed." They started making out. After a while, they simply held each other.

"Jethro, after that mammogram showed no sign of cancer, we both knew that God had done something special in us that first time we prayed together that special way at Deborah's."

He nodded. "I cannot imagine my future without you."

"So, are you saying you want me to be your wife?"

"Exactly. Would you like to have a big show-business-style wedding, or can we just invite family members to meet us at the church one Saturday?"

"How about this coming Saturday morning? The one person other than family, and in addition to Pastor Jerry and his wife Pam, is that I want Deborah to be there."

He nodded. "I agree. If you want to call her, I'll go and fix us some hot chocolate." He got up and went to his kitchen.

Alice pressed a speed-dial button on her phone. "Hey, Pam! Jethro and I want to get married this Saturday in a small wedding with just family and possibly one or two friends. Is Pastor Jerry handy?"

"Sure! He'll be here in a moment." It took less than a minute.

"Hi, Deborah! So, you and Jethro want a small wedding ceremony on Saturday? We can do that! Is there a reason for the rush?"

"No, Jethro and I have a godly relationship, but why wait?"

"Okay. What time?"

Alice closed her eyes briefly. "Let's make it 10:00, okay?"

"All right. I must say, I'm not surprised."

"I am, but my heart says it is time. I'll call you again in a day or two. Bye."

"Bye, Alice."

She pushed another speed-dial button.

"Hi, Alice! What's up?"

"Jethro and I have decided to invite our families to the church on Saturday morning and get married. We want you to be there, Deborah."

"Wow! Terrific!"

"I also want to invite you into a wondrous conspiracy with me."

"Tell me!"

"Jethro was talking with Saul, and he asked him if there was any possibility of romance between him and Jess, the neighbor that's watching over him under General Plummer's orders."

"And...."

"Saul said he's attracted to her, but that she's half his age, while he's a confirmed bachelor, so they'll never get married."

"Hang on a minute, Alice." She was in her kitchen, and she knelt on the floor beside the counter and closed her eyes. Images flashed through her mind. She stood up again and picked up her phone. "Alice, Jess is a warrior that God has been preparing. Invite Saul to come and tell him he must call General Plummer for security reasons. The General will tell Jess to go as Saul's wedding 'date.' I'll talk to Jess before the wedding. All that God does, God does well, Alice."

"Yes, He certainly does. I'll talk with you again in a few days. Bye."

"Bye, Alice."

Jethro walked in from his kitchen with steaming mugs of hot chocolate. Alice filled him in about her conversations with Pastor Jerry and Deborah. The next day, they would be making many calls.

Deborah played her harp for the wedding, and the rest of *New Rocks* was there for dance music at the reception. Jethro and Alice started the first dance, and then others began to join them.

At first, Saul and Jess watched from their table. Then Jess stood up and held out her hand. "Come on, Saul, let's join them."

"I'm not much of a dancer."

"That's okay, it's a special occasion." They went out onto the dance area. They looked at each other as they were dancing. "I don't know why you said you're not much of a dancer. I think you're a good dancer."

"Do you think so, Jess?"

She kissed him. "Definitely."

He kissed her back, and their kiss continued through the rest of that dance number.

Chapter Nine
Government Transformation Begins

After many months of posting confrontational emails exposing federal government corruption, along with corruption in many state governments, the project was coming nearly to completion. Deborah was still posting to her blog *What Lies Ahead*. She had begun the blog before the confrontations project, and she planned to continue. She began to prepare her blog's viewers for the next phase.

> *Many months before the confrontation emails began, I began to warn my viewers that a cleanup of government was coming. The wisdom of our founding fathers began to reassert itself over the last several months. It was John Adams who said,* **"Our constitution was made only for a moral and religious people. It is wholly inadequate to the government of any other."** *Contrary to the political lies often told in recent years, most Christians in this country have never wanted a theocracy.*

She then went on to predict the hard work that lies ahead in the aftermath of the cleanup.

In the next day's video conference, Jethro, Saul, and Fred wanted to discuss what Deborah had said in the blog. Jethro led off the discussion. "Almost everything you said we've discussed in small portions, but when you put it all in one 400-word blog post, it was almost overwhelming."

"Indeed." Saul was adamant. "I'm glad we've agreed to profile all the candidates for major offices during this presidential election year. Still, Deborah, I would like to see you post your reactions to statements made by the candidates, particularly those that draw the most media attention."

Fred was nodding. "Yeah. We've established a reputation for telling the truth, so let's continue to hold the media's feet to the fire." He paused. "Jethro, I suggest that you start a blog entitled *Hacker Dude Reports*. Wearing your John Wayne Mask. You've already established the character with Nicholas Terry. Just as James Maffett used to help Deborah, maybe Alice might be able to help you."

Jethro smiled. "What do you think, Deborah? Might this be a new role for my bride to play in the background?"

She nodded. "Perhaps." She smiled. "The last of the confrontation emails will be posted a week from Friday. There's time to think about it and pray about it between now and then."

The following week, on the Friday night the final confrontation email went out, Deborah had a vividly colorful dream. When her alarm went off, she picked up her phone and called Alice. "Good morning, Deborah! Jethro is still asleep, but I've been memorizing lines for a new script for the last couple of hours. If you're calling me this early, God must have given you a dream, right?"

"Yes, my friend. It involved both you and Jethro."

"Really! Tell me!"

"You need to help Jethro resurrect Hacker Dude, as was discussed a couple of weeks ago. The reason you need to be involved is because on Sunday at noon, Alexandra Peterson, the Governor of Oregon, is going to announce that she is running for President." [Also seen in *Elijah* © 2020]

"You're kidding! I've known Alex for several years. She and I have shared the dais on talk shows several times. She's a fine Christian woman."

"Yes, she is. You'll need to help Jethro prepare his blog because he'll need a woman's perspective on the presidency from you, and he'll need to pick your brain regarding your friendship with Alex."

Wearing his bathrobe, Jethro walked into the home office where Alice was studying her lines and now on the phone. He softly said, "Who?"

"Deborah, Jethro is awake, and he just walked into the office, where I'm talking with you. Do you want to tell him what you've told me?"

"No, I need to get started on my scripture readings and my morning prayers time. Just tell him that it's important to post the first of his new blogs by this evening, before Alex makes her announcement."

"Okay. Bye, Deborah."

"Bye."

Alice stood up and held out her arms. "Good morning, Jethro." They hugged for a while, and after a lingering kiss she said, "Deborah's call was for both of us, but you were still asleep the last time I looked."

"I heard Deborah's ringtone on your phone. What's up?

Alice filled him in with all the details, and then she added, "I met Alex when she was running for Governor the first time. We're kind of fans of each other. Her husband, Tom, is a great guy, too."

"Okay. Let's start writing out what I should say in my first blog after we have some breakfast, read our scriptures, and pray. I need to come up with a name for my blog. I didn't like Fred's suggestion. You go ahead with studying your script. I'll get dressed before I start breakfast. I'll call you when its ready."

After breakfast, it was late morning when he was finally satisfied with what they had written. "What kind of background do you think John Wayne / Hacker Dude should have?"

Alice was thoughtful. "Whatever we decide, you should use the same – or nearly the same – background for each post of your blog. Since that end of our office," she pointed, "is chroma-key green, you can pose as though you are in whatever location you want."

Jethro nodded. "With my John Wayne persona, my first impulse is to put him somewhere in the southwest with a ranch background or something scenic like the Grand Canyon." He paused, closed his eyes, and breathed deeply.

She didn't speak again until he opened his eyes. "I assume you were praying just now, but if you were communing with God like Deborah does, you and I need to pray with each other and for each other more."

He nodded. "I apologize, my darling. Give me your hands." He held them out, and she grasped them. Let's seek God's presence. If God gives you something to say, say it, and I'll do the same."

They were silent for the better part of five minutes when simultaneously they opened their eyes and spoke together. "Washington D.C.!"

She was excited. "It should be a different public location every time. Can we make it current?"

Jethro grinned. "With so many cameras in that city? It'll be a cinch!" He paused. I've got to make this a positive blog, so I think I'll call it, *A Hacker's Hopes.* "I'll go put on my mask, voice enhancer, and a Pendleton shirt. Have you ever thought about the fact that Deborah always is seen on camera in clothing made in this country?"

Alice was thoughtful. "I hadn't thought about it but, yes, you're right!"

"I think I'll try to at least use clothing of American brands."

"Good idea. While you put on your voice disk and face mask, I'll search Washington for a background for you that has only a few in view, hopefully none. We won't want other people in the scene to be recognizable. I want something else too."

"What's that?"

"I'm going to send a tweet to my fan clubs and tell them to check out a new blog called *A Hacker's Hopes.* Are you going to create accounts in all the social media?"

"Of course. For me, that'll only take a few minutes. You do your thing while I'll do mine."

The media started reporting the new blog called *A Hacker's Hopes* that evening. UBN made a point of Hacker Dude's previous appearance with Nicholas Terry. Nicholas said that he would try to bring Hacker Dude back for another interview. All of them mentioned that Hacker Dude hoped that one of the candidates for President would be a governor of one of the west coast states.

When Alexandra Peterson announced that she was running for President the next morning, she was asked whether she knew that during the previous evening, Hacker Dude expressed his hope that a West Coast governor would run for President. She smiled. "I've had no communication with Hacker Dude. Several years ago, I had a conversation with the Texas prophet named Elijah, but I've never spoken with this man. If I do, I'll thank him for what he said last evening."

During the weeks that followed, Democrats, Independents, and Republicans announced their candidacies. As more and more people were announcing that they were running for state political offices, several of them mentioned being inspire d by Alexandra Peterson.

Two days after the first *A Hacker's Hopes* blog entry, Deborah called for a teleconference with the team. "Jethro's blog has stimulated politicians throughout the country. It seems to me that we need to confine our team's output to presidential candidates, vice-presidential candidates, and candidates for governor."

Jethro nodded. "Also, our efforts should not be overtly focused upon corruption. I think we should focus upon positive support of the good stuff, and we should only mention past negative behaviors and speeches in passing."

"Indeed." Saul Wolfe concurred. "I was talking to General Plummer yesterday, and he said that he hopes that the media will spend at least **some** time reporting positive aspects of the campaigns ahead."

Fred was curious. "I don't recall seeing any real dirt on Alexandra Peterson or her husband or kids."

Jethro nodded. "California's governor, Jerry Newton, used to say nasty things about Governor Peterson, but then he became a Christian himself, and now they are friends. Tom Peterson has raised a lot of money for the Lions Clubs International SightFirst programs. He seems to genuinely enjoy being a do-gooder. Still, I checked our database this morning, and it has lots of material on the Petersons. Fred, your group needs to start creating files on all the candidates for major offices that we have not already compiled."

Fred nodded. "We'll tackle each one as they announce they are running. Saul, have you any idea who Governor Peterson might choose as her running mate?"

"No. We can't expect any hint of that until after the primary season."

Deborah was thoughtful. "Okay, everyone, it seems we all have a sense of the challenges ahead. Unless there's major news, let's plan our next teleconference for two weeks from today." All of them disconnected. She closed her eyes in prayer for several minutes.

Opening her eyes, she took out her phone and pressed a speed-dial button. "Good morning, Mom. I'm thinking of heading out for *The Breakfast Bar* on Atlantic Avenue. Have you and Dad got any plans for lunch?"

"That sounds great. I was just beginning to think about fixing sandwiches. What time shall we meet you there? We can probably get there in fifteen minutes."

"If I leave right now, I can be there by 11:30 or so."

"We'll be there. Bye! ...George!" She hung up.

There was no traffic, so Deborah already had a table when her parents got there. She stood up and greeted them with hugs. "I felt like having lunch out, and I thought you might too."

George smiled at his daughter. "We needed to get out of the house for a while anyway. What's new"

A waiter approached with glasses of water, and they placed their orders. He left.

Alexandra touched her daughter's hand. "I've been wondering. Do you think anything is going to develop between you and David?"

"No, that's not going to happen, Mom. A couple of weeks ago, Jethro and Alice brought a friend of hers to church. Her name is Amber Hough. Alice introduced Amber to David, and it was like fireworks going off between them. They've been seeing each other every day since then."

Her Mom smiled. "If they're serious, Deborah, how do you feel about that?"

"I'm happy for them. I've never had romantic feelings for David."

Her Dad interrupted. "Is there anything new going on with your team?"

Deborah looked around and saw no one was nearby to listen. She lowered her voice. "Candidates for major offices are getting profiled more rigorously than the media have done in many years. By any chance, have you seen the new blog called *A Hacker's Hopes*?" It puts a positive spin on this election year."

Her Dad lowered his voice to match hers. "Do you know Hacker Dude?"

Deborah smiled sweetly. "No comment, Dad."

Her Mom looked at her. "Really? That's your answer?"

"You know me as well as anyone, Mom."

Their waiter approached with their meals.

At that moment in Palos Verdes Estates, Alice was almost jumping up and down with excitement. "You've gotten tens of thousands of hits, Jethro! You already have almost ten thousand followers!"

He smiled. "It's probably because I'm putting a positive spin on politics after years of political corruption." He hugged her. "On another subject, how did the casting interview go down in Austin? Our home seemed so empty while you were gone yesterday."

"I'm going to play a supporting role as an unnamed angel who appears from time to time throughout the movie. During the hero's more than four hundred years of life, he outlives wife after wife. [*An Extensive Life* © 2017]."

Jethro nodded. "I know. While you were gone yesterday, I read it. I didn't finish it until after midnight, but I wanted to be able to discuss the plot with you while knowing what you are going to be talking about. I like the way the story is wrapped up."

"The angel's part is a small one, but I'm just getting started in the Christian film industry. I'll get bigger parts with more experiences."

Jethro nodded. "I know. Sometimes I think that the secular entertainment industry is as corrupt as our country's politics used to be. Speaking of politics, some of the dirtiest media blogs are already doing their 'investigative' pieces on these first men and women to throw their hats into the presidential ring. Saul has emailed me some suggestions for my next blog. I'm always open to your suggestions, you know."

She kissed his cheek. "Yes. There have been some wonderful German satirists that have skewered yellow journalism. I'll see if I can come up with some good examples." She paused. "My first appearances in this production will be shot in Scotland and Wales. Do you want to go with me?"

He grinned. "Of course! A long time ago, I learned from Admiral Rockwell that the next time he and his wife go to Wales, Deborah wants to go with them. Maybe we can make a place for them near one of your production locations."

Alice smiled. "Let's make it happen!"

It was the second week in June when a week's production was started in Scotland. Guest starring was Daniel Dench as James VI of Scotland for a brief scene. Jerry and Becky Rockwell were with Deborah, sitting quietly nearby as the scene was being shot. There was a moment when, between takes, Daniel Dench spotted Deborah. He approached the group. "Excuse me, but are you the guests of Alice Schiffer? I'm Daniel Dench."

They all introduced themselves. The Admiral explained their presence. "Becky and I have seen quite a bit of the British Isles, and Deborah has always wanted to see Wales, so when Alice told us that she was going to shoot two scenes over here, we invited Deborah to tag along."

Daniel smiled. "It's nice to meet you all. I hope all of us can have lunch together later." He looked across the set. "I must get back in place. Please excuse me."

Over lunch, Daniel listened attentively to Jerry and Becky, with their tales of his being on the Joint Chiefs of Staff. He thought Deborah was fascinating, and mentally resolved to get to know her. She though that he wasn't a stuffy as she expected, but she wasn't aware of his admiration for her.

While they were there in the British Isles, both Deborah and Jethro continued to post to their blogs, though their video backgrounds were just video clips on their hard drives. Jethro used images of Washington, and Deborah seemed to be taking a vacation in Yosemite. The second appearance of the angel was shot on the west coast of Wales. Since the rest of the movie was being shot in Texas and northern California, Alice, Jethro, Deborah, and the others flew back the following Friday. The five of them fought off jet lag on Saturday.

On Sunday they all returned to Ximeno Christian Church, and they were surprised to see Daniel Dench there. After church, Deborah began to realize that Daniel was smitten with her. She was puzzled. She was so recently widowed, she wasn't ready for him. Daniel returned to London on that Tuesday.

Several weeks went by. Deborah miscarried. She spent the night in the Emergency Room at Seaside Hospital. Her Mom and Dad joined her less than a half hour after she got there. To her surprise, she felt at peace.

Her Mom was concerned. "It looks like you've already put your miscarriage behind you. Why?"

Her Dad nodded. "Yes, why? I would have expected a strong negative or at least sad reaction from you."

Deborah sighed. "It's like I've been holding on to James, with part of him inside me. Now, it's like I'm turning a page in my personal life. I will always have precious memories of James, but now I can move ahead into the future God has prepared for me." She went home the next afternoon.

The team continued to post their profiles of the candidates at a steady pace, often setting the record straight in response to yellow journalism. During the first presidential debate, everyone on Deborah's team made detailed notes on their own responses to the candidates' statements. They also made notes on the questions from the media.

That night, Deborah had another colorful dream. During breakfast, she constantly pondered the dream. In the dream, she saw the results of the election, and she knew that the team that she and Jethro had formed would have much more work to do.

After dealing with the dishes, she fixed herself a mug of hot chocolate and went into the great room to pray. Sitting in a recliner and looking out the great room's windows, she discussed it aloud with God for most of the morning.

Abruptly, Deborah's grief resurfaced. Tears began to run down her cheeks. It was a clear day, with no visible smog or fog. She could see all Catalina Island. Memories of her trips to the town of Avalon there with James came flooding back to her. James had loved going out on the glass-bottomed boat with her. They loved seeing the under-water marine life.

Then she had memories of going diving with James in La Jolla, just north of San Diego. They had brought home several Abalone and had steaks from those shellfish. Following a recipe given to her by her mother, they both found that those sea snails are delicious. The shells were great for decorating their bookshelves.

Growing sleepy, Deborah took a nap.

Chapter Ten
Election Aftermath

On election night, Nicholas Terry was the news anchor throughout the night at Los Angeles station KUBN. Deborah, Jethro, and Alice watched together in her great room on her large monitor.

As soon as the polls closed in Hawaii, the election was called. "We have a clear winner, everyone. Alexandra Peterson will be our next President, and Joshua Baird will be our next Vice President." Nicholas Terry was tired, but he was professional and poised. "During our next hour, former California governor, Jerry Newton, will be here. He knows the President-elect and her husband very well. First, however, we will switch to our Washington Bureau, where Judy Brock of the White House press corps offers us an interview she did earlier today with our current President. Here's Judy Brock."

As the Judy Brock interview began, Deborah lowered the volume, and Alice was excited. "I'm so happy for Alex! After her inauguration next month, I'll put a call in to the White House and see if I can meet her for lunch."

Jethro grinned, "I hope you take me with you! I've never talked with a President before. I've always just criticized them from the sidelines."

Deborah spoke quietly. "It will be interesting to see how she deals with the White House Press Corps. Her new press secretary is Carol Ann McPherson, who is very capable, but the President will probably hold a press conference soon after she's established in the Oval Office."

Jethro nodded. "Our team has prepared large and detailed packages of coverage of both the Petersons and the Bairds. Joshua Baird was a typical politician in his days as Pennsylvania's Governor, telling about as many lies as most, but when our confrontations began, he was one of the first to own up to his faults and clean up his administration. It was impressive repentance, and so far, he's been rather clean since. Time will tell, of course."

Deborah nodded. "I want to tell the two of you something personal. It seems like eons ago I told you that James had gotten me pregnant before he was killed. A couple of days ago I miscarried."

Alice put her arms around her, and Jethro put an arm across their shoulders. Alice spoke softly. "I'm so sorry, my friend!"

"I'm kind of okay with it. I've turned a page in my personal life." They talked about it for more than an hour.

Early in the campaign, the team had prepared a large and detailed package of coverage of the Petersons, with all the data clearly verified. The package included rarely seen videos, going back all the way to Sam and Alex's wedding. The package went out to hundreds of media outlets less than a half hour after the winner had been declared.

For most of the week, the media focused primarily on the winners of the election. Deborah's team posted three or four profiles of the winning governors every night. With each profile, the media's coverage of the races was reviewed through video files Jethro accessed from his access to *Political Nightmares* and a few new sources.

To Jethro's surprise, a new trend developed. The major media outlets began critiquing themselves and each other. They were ruthless! Saul's and Fred's teams posted files on the media demonstrating both their accuracies and their inaccuracies. Saul was thoroughly enjoying himself. Fred's team members aid many times that it was fun.

Alice supplied Jethro some suggestions for satire of the continuing yellow journalism that was beginning to wane slightly. Alice was brilliant at adapting some historic German satire for use by her husband. During their devotions and prayer time together, they spent some time contemplating how God was melting and molding her.

Alexandra Peterson's inauguration speech was unlike that of her predecessor. It was nearly an hour long, but she made several points of interest to Deborah and Jethro.

- *The evening before I announced my intention to run for President, an Internet personality named 'Hacker Dude' posted his first blog, and I'd like to meet him one day.*

- *The night after I announced my candidacy, the hackers that exposed political corruption in our country posted a package of files on me that were almost embarrassingly accurate. I owe them a debt of thanks, so thank you!*

- *There's a prophet who looks like a descendent of the late Audrey Hepburn who seems to know what is going on in Washington before anyone else does. I'd like to talk with her one day.*

- *When so much of the corruption was being exposed, my husband Sam and I read all the files that came from the hackers. From those files I learned who I can trust, and from the list I complied I have asked them to be in my cabinet and on my staff.*

Alexandra and Sam Peterson went to all the inaugural balls. She wore something different for each ball, but the new First Gentleman consistently looked dashing in a traditional black tux.

That night, God gave Deborah another dream. In the dream, she knew that God was once again going to use her like Phillip the Evangelist in the Bible's book of Acts. Knowing that there was quite a bit of snow on the ground in Washington, D.C., she knew she had to dress for heavy snow even though she was in Southern California in her home.

As she got dressed, memories flooded back to her of going to Yosemite for Christmas with James one year. She and James had marveled at huge flakes that they saw falling there when they spent a day at the Badger Pass. This time, by the time she finished breakfast and put her dishes in the dishwasher, she was ready, wearing a long winter coat, with her snow boots, muffler, and winter cap.

Just like it happened previously, Deborah vanished from her kitchen only to find herself sitting on the steps of the Lincoln Memorial. It was cold and mid-morning in the Eastern Time Zone. Big flakes of snow were falling. In the distance, she could see a horse mounted Police Officer.

As she began walking towards the White House, Deborah's were the only footprints in the snow that was falling steadily, as far as she could see. When she reached the guardhouse at the gate to the grounds, the officer immediately recognized her. "Good morning. I'll tell reception that the blogger of *What Lies Ahead* is here to see the President, am I correct?"

Deborah nodded. "That's correct. Thank you for remembering me."

"Yes, Ma'am." He picked up his phone. "The blogger of *What Lies Ahead* is here to see the President." He paused to listen. "Yes, sir." He looked at her and smiled. "They are ready to receive you."

She returned his smile. "Thank you."

In less than a minute, she was enjoying the warmth inside the White House. The new Press Secretary was signing in, and she greeted her. "Good morning! I know that you are the blogger of *What Lies Ahead,* but I don't know that you have ever revealed your name. I'm Carol Ann McPherson."

There was a nudge deep within her. "Between you and me, my name is Deborah."

"It's a pleasure to meet you. I'll take you to the outer office to the President. If you wish, you can leave your coat, muffler, and cap here. Security will keep an eye on them for you."

As they walked together, a few greeted Carol Ann, but most people in the hallway barely glanced at Deborah in her Audrey Hepburn mask. The Oval Office's secretary stood and greeted her. "Good morning. It's an honor to meet you. I've read every one of your blog posts for as long as I can remember. " There was a buzz from her desk, and she stepped away from her desk to open a door. "You can go right in."

"Thank you."

The President walked towards her with her hand extended. "Good morning! This is amazing! A few days ago, in my inaugural address, I mentioned that I wanted to talk with you, and here you are."

"Good morning, Madam President. It's a pleasure to meet you as well."

"Let's sit down. If you're hungry, I can have our chef prepare anything you'd like."

Deborah's grin stretched her mask a little. "No thank you. You're approaching lunch time now. You have the excellent habit of sharing a meal during important meetings. You could do that in your Governor's mansion, but there are too many important meetings here to make that practical. May I assume that you will not share much of this conversation except as absolutely necessary and in confidence with your staff?"

President Peterson nodded. "If that is your wish, I will honor it. Getting down to today's business, are you familiar with my choices for cabinet positions and staff?"

"Yes. You've made good choices, though all of us are sinners, so mistakes will be made. The senate will approve your Cabinet, although a few Senators will swallow hard when they vote to approve. You can be sure you'll have difficulty with learning to trust some of the leaders in our bureaucracy. To that end, I offer you a suggestion. First, however, why don't you invite your Chief of Staff, Donna Young, to join us and take notes."

Alexandra smiled, stood up, and walked to another door than the one where Deborah entered. "So, you evidently trust Donna Young."

"Yes." Deborah stood up to greet the Chief of Staff. "Good morning! I suggested that you join us, so a transcript of this meeting won't be necessary."

Donna nodded. "Good morning." They shook hands. "Thank you for trusting me." The three of them sat down, and the President summarized what Deborah had said up until that point.

Deborah nodded. "You will no doubt wonder here at the beginning how much you can trust the leaders of our intelligence agencies. None of them have perfect track records, and the FBI's record has some serious blots on their trustworthiness. Commendably, they are trying to put all that into uncomfortable old history."

The President nodded and sighed. "You said you have a suggestion."

"Yes. The first is a man who lives in Mentor on the Lake, Ohio. Saul Wolfe, of Wolfe Investigations, is brilliant, he's totally ethical and trustworthy, he has amazing resources, and he is a devout Christian. If you ask him to investigate one or two specific people, he might do it gratis, though he normally charges exceedingly high fees. His answer will come to your private email address in an encrypted file. Your password will be the day of the week followed by the city and state of your first date with Sam."

President Peterson burst out laughing. "Wonderful!" Donna had a wry smile, and she didn't write it down.

Deborah continued. "Depending on Wolfe's circumstances when you make your request, there is a chance that Wolfe will invite another investigator into the process. His name is Fred Drake, of Port St. Lucie, Florida. Just between us, both Wolfe and Drake sometimes find themselves able to utilize the resources of the man known as Hacker Dude. You may be familiar with his blog called, *A Hacker's Hopes.*" Both the President and her Chief of Staff nodded.

Deborah continued. "You've probably noticed how many in the media are trying to clean up their reputations as well as their behavior. There are still problems with corruption and yellow journalism. What I'm about to tell you is strictly between us, and possibly with Carol Ann McPherson, your Press

Secretary that I met when I arrived. A woman has recently rejoined the White House Press Corps after living in Florida and getting married. Her name is Judy Brock. [*Elijah* © 2020] She's smart as a whip, and she has little if any political bias of her own. She might be a reliable resource for you."

Donna was curious. "Why did she leave the Press Corps? Was it because of her husband?"

Deborah shook her head. "She lived with her sister in Pensacola during the nuclear winter." She paused. "While we are talking about trustworthy people in the media, I should mention one more person. He's a UBN correspondent named Nicholas Terry. He's politically neutral, and he follows the truth wherever it may lead him. He may well be as smart as Saul Wolfe."

Donna nodded. "Nicholas Terry interviewed me right after I was appointed here. I liked him, and I instinctively knew I could trust him."

Deborah smiled. "In your inaugural address." Madam President, "you mentioned Hacker Dude. I seriously doubt that he would be willing to sit down with you as I am. He likes to work behind the scenes, assisting other people. He got married recently, so that might change. Do you have any questions while I'm here today?"

The President nodded. "During the previous administration, you were listed in the Visitors Log for a while, and then that entry disappeared. Is there anything you can tell me about that?"

Deborah smiled. "A while ago I walked from the Lincoln Memorial to the Guard House out in front while it was snowing with some big and fluffy flakes. The guard at the gate, whose name I know to be Adrian, recognized me, and we exchanged pleasantries. When I leave, I'll probably go back in the same direction. I enjoyed that beautiful walk in the snow." She paused. "I must be going now. Donna, will you please escort me back to the entrance?"

Donna looked at her boss, who nodded. "Sure. I'll be glad to."

They stood up, and the President shook Deborah's hand again. "I'm glad you came today. You've been immensely helpful."

The prophet nodded. "I am also glad I came. I've enjoyed meeting both of you." Donna led the way as she and Deborah left the office. As they were walking down a hallway, Deborah spoke softly to her. "Don't worry about that lump you discovered on your upper thigh when you took a shower last evening. It's gone."

Donna's eyes grew wide. "You're serious?"

Deborah nodded. "Of course, Donna." They said their farewells as Deborah put her muffler, coat, and cap back on.

Outside, it was more of the big and fluffy flakes. At the guard house she said, "It was good to see you again, Adrian. Bye"

"It was good to see you as well, Ma'am. Bye!" A thought occurred to him, and his eyes grew wide. He thought, *She knows my name!*

Deborah went through the gate and turned. She did not see anyone else, and there was only one taxi in the distance. After walking about a block, she pulled part of her muffler up from under her coat and over her mouth. Suddenly, she was in her garage on Signal Hill, just outside her kitchen door. She stomped her boots to get the accumulation of snow off them, and then she hung her coat, muffler, and cap on the rack next to the door. She was home.

Taking out her phone, she pressed a speed-dial button. "Hi, Jethro. I'm calling because God took me to see our new President this morning. I met the new Press Secretary, Carol Ann McPherson. She will be a major asset to the new administration."

"We have very little on her in our files."

"No, that's true. She's a granddaughter of an excellent old-world-style politician, who passed away while she was getting her degree in journalism."

"I'll see what I can find out about her. You had a good talk with Alexandra Peterson?"

"Yes. Just after we started chatting, I suggested that she have her new Chief of Staff, Donna Young, to join us. You mentioned her a few times in our conferences during the campaign. I like her."

"Yes, she's quite impressive."

"I suggested Saul and Fred as possible investigative sources when she has questions about people in the bureaucracy. Because she mentioned you in her inaugural address, I told her that I doubted she would be able to meet you because of your desire to be a background person. I also told her that you had gotten married recently, so that your attitude might change."

Jethro chuckled. "You know me so well, Deborah."

"She asked about my previously recorded visit to the White House in the previous administration, telling me that my visit was no longer on the record."

"How did you handle it?"

"I was a bit coy. I told her that I enjoyed walking in the snow, hinted that the Guard at the gate recognized me today, and told Madam President that I knew the guard's name."

"So, do you think it was a fruitful visit?"

"The President indicated that it was for her, and it was for me as well."

Chapter Eleven
New Life & Fresh Days

The daily alarm for Jethro and Alice was programmed into the video screen mounted on their bedroom ceiling. One Wednesday morning, when the UBN headlines came on, Jethro rubbed his eyes as Alice came out of their master bath with a big smile. "Jethro! Guess what?"

"What?"

"We're pregnant!" She shouted it out and began jumping up and down.

He jumped out of bed and wrapped her in his arms. "Terrific!" He kissed her passionately.

When they broke for air, she jumped back onto the bed. "After breakfast, I'll call Dr. McCormack. First, our devotions, right?"

"Right! I'd like to take the time to read the first eight chapters of Romans this morning. How about it?"

"Sure! The last time I read through Romans, I was on location for a movie in Santorini." She paused. "Later, let's have waffles for breakfast."

"Okay."

Nearly 2400 miles northeast of there by car, Saul was putting on his overcoat and gloves. Both he and Jess were excited that her pregnancy test came back positive. "I wish I could go with you to see Dr. Osherowitz, but...."

Jess nodded. "I know. You've got tons of work to do. I'll call you when I'm done. I want to call Deborah and tell her we're preggers. She's become such a good friend."

"Okay. I'll see you at Nate's for lunch at noon."

"Right. Nate's. See ya!" She blew him a kiss.

Saul went into their garage. He and Jess had gotten pregnant at almost the same time as Alice and Jethro.

Deborah, however, had decided that she needed a vacation. The team's activities had slowed down to taking their actions only once or twice a week. Deborah felt she could finally get away. Most of Saul's and Fred's operatives were working on other projects.

Deborah flew out of the Long Beach Airport to San Francisco on a Monday afternoon for the short flight there. Rather than rent a car, she relied on public transportation as most visitors to the Bay Area do. She stayed in the Lodge at the Presidio. After checking in, she went to the Concierge. "Good afternoon. I'm Deborah Maffett. I'm going to spend a week or so here in the Bay Area. I want to spend tomorrow spending at least a half day with someone who lives here, who can take me on a personalized tour."

He smiled. "My name is Samuel, I'll be glad to help you with that excellent choice. What time would you like to leave in the morning?"

"I'm an early riser. I can probably finish having breakfast before 8:00."

"Very good. I'll have a car here to pick you up and take you on a tour at 8:00. They will be flexible regarding what interests you. Since you're doing it by the hour, you will be charged as such, which will be added to your bill here."

"That will be fine. Shall I come to this desk at 8:00?"

"Yes, Mrs. Maffett. That will be good."

Deborah silenced her phone and had a good night's sleep. Her phone beeped twice while she was taking a shower the next morning, and after she got dressed, she decided to check for calls before going on her tour. Both Alice and Jess left voicemail messages telling her about their pregnancies. Deborah looked at her watch. It was nearly 8:00 AM, so returning the calls would have to wait until she finished her tour of San Francisco.

She enjoyed the entire day. The sun was setting when her tour guide dropped her off at the Lodge. Deborah enjoyed watching the sunset as she ate at a table by a window in the Commissary.

Returning to her room, she took out her phone and called. Alice. "Deborah! Tell me all about your day in the city by the bay!"

"It was terrific, my friend. I didn't get back to here at the Lodge at the Presidio until just as the sun was beginning to set. I had dinner in the Commissary. What does your doctor say? When are you due?"

"So far. Jess and I are going to give birth at about the same time. We're both about two months along. Have you talked with her?"

"No, I got voice mails from both of you, and I just happened to call you first. I'm going to take the BART under the bay tomorrow to Oakland. You know the east side of the bay rather well. Is there anything you think that I simply must visit?"

"The wonderful surprise for me and Jethro was a church founded by the late Frank Frazee and his second wife. It's up in the Oakland Hills, it's called Hilltop Christian Center, and it is huge and graceful." [Also seen in *A Second Call to Serve.* © 2018]

"The Lodge here has an excellent Concierge. I'm sure he can give me directions on how to get there. On the other hand, I'll have to take a taxi from the BART station, so I'm sure he'll know." Deborah and Alice talked another fifteen minutes, and then she returned Jess' call.

"Hi, Jess! This is Deborah calling from San Francisco."

"Hi! Have you talked to Alice yet?"

"Yes, I just talked with her. It looks like the two of you will have your first children at about the same time, about seven months from now."

"Yes! I've resigned from the Naval Reserves. God is so good! The next day I was able to get a job as the new Chief of Security at TriPoint Medical Center. One of the benefits is that I have free health care. General Plummer put in a phone call, and the job almost fell into my lap."

"Praise God! How's Saul?"

"Right now, he's still at the office, but each evening he and I are working on converting one of our bedrooms to a nursery, and we're going to convert another bedroom to a playroom in a year or two. He should be getting home soon. How's the weather up there in Northern California?"

"It's pretty cool here, but I'm going to Oakland tomorrow, and the forecast there is for sunshine."

"I was stationed in Monterey for a while. Northern California weather can be unpredictable. San Francisco only seemed to be sunny in September, but the East Bay area seemed to have more definite seasons. Right now, I've got to fire up our barbeque. I'm fixing steaks for a late dinner. Call me after you go up into the wine country, okay?"

"I'll do it, Jess. Say hello to Saul for me."

"I will. Bye." Deborah picked up the hotel phone handset and dialed the Concierge Desk. She recognized the man's voice. "Good evening, Samuel, this is Deborah Maffett. Thank you for arranging my private escorted tour of the city today. Tomorrow, I'll be taking the BART to Oakland, and I plan to spend the day there, unless I take the BART further east. I'd like for you to arrange an escorted tour of the wine country for me."

"I'm glad you enjoyed today's tour. We can arrange for wine country tours for up to three days or more, or you can spend just a single day. What is your preference?"

"I've been wanting to see that area for a long time. What do you recommend?"

They discussed the possibilities, and Deborah decided on a two-day tour that sounded scenic as well as fun. The next morning, she enjoyed a leisurely breakfast in her room, and then she took a taxi to the nearest BART station. Deborah was surprised at how quiet and fast the train was. She got off at the second Oakland station, where there were two taxis waiting for customers.

After getting in, she said, I'm told there is a big church up in the Oakland Hills that is named Hilltop Christian Center, that was founded by the late Frank Frazee. Do you know where it is?"

"Yes, Ma'am. I'm a deacon there. We can be there in less than ten minutes." He put his flag down, and they were under way. "The pastor who replaced Frank Frazee when he retired is retiring next year. His name is Elmer Hanson. He was here during the nuclear winter, of course." The driver talked as he drove. "I joined the church during the nuclear winter. Nothing seemed to slow us down as a congregation – not the cold or the snow. When my wife and I first visited, we knew that it was to be our church home." A few minutes later, he pulled into the church parking lot.

"Thank you. On your license I see that your name is John Cummings. What's your wife's name?"

"Her name's Angel."

"I'll add you and your wife to my prayer list, John." She paid the fare and added a generous tip. "Thanks again." She got out.

Looking about, she took in the size of one large building. It looked like a large hotel, only there were not as many windows as a hotel would have. Deborah was dumbfounded. Seeing double doors to what was apparently the entrance, she walked in that direction and went inside.

The foyer was very spacious. Off to her right, an older man was approaching. "Good morning. I'm Elmer Hanson, the pastor of Hilltop Christian Center. I'm guessing that you are Deborah Maffett. Admiral Jerry Rockwell called me this morning."

She was stunned. "My friend named Jethro must have called him."

"I don't know about that. I got to know the Admiral and his wife, Becky, during the nuclear winter. They worshipped with us a number of times when he was stationed at the Hunters Point Naval Shipyard." He paused. Would you like to see our sanctuary?"

"Yes, please. Coming inside, the décor is not at all what I expected, based upon the outside façade."

Elmer smiled. "Yes, almost everyone notices that. The architect was Leroy Wright." He opened a door into the worship area. Once again, Deborah was stunned. It was spacious and beautiful, like the inside of a giant log cabin. Elmer pointed out some of the features. "Those large wood beams hide most of the lighting and all the technology we need in a modern church. The video screen is 8K, which is ample for our needs. It eliminates the need to have a projector and screen."

Deborah nodded. "The architecture is magnificent. I heard your predecessor, Frank Frazee, preach on our video feed down in Long Beach, when I was growing up. I remember him as being incredibly dynamic."

"For me, he was a good friend. He was in his fiftieth year of preaching the first time I preached here." Elmer paused as he looked at his watch. "I'm expecting a pastor friend of mine to be here in about a half hour. His name is Zhang Jie. Being Chinese, his first name comes after his family name. He became a widower last year when his wife died of cancer. Now, I'm helping him find another church because he wants to get away from this area where there are so many memories."

Deborah felt a nudge deep within her as she stared at a cross near the front of the church. "Elmer, one of the things that my late husband and I used to say is, "All that God does, God does well."

"Interesting! Frank and Debra Sue used to say the same thing."

The door where they came in opened again, and a Chinese man entered. He looked ageless. "Good morning, Elmer! Who is your friend?"

"Good morning, Al. This is Deborah Maffett. She is visiting from the Long Beach area."

She smiled. "Good morning! It is a pleasure to meet you! I just told Elmer that one of my favorite sayings is, 'All that God does, God does well.' He said that it was also the favorite saying of the founding pastor and his wife. I understand that your wife graduated to heaven recently."

He shook Deborah's hand. "It is a genuine pleasure to meet you, Deborah. Yes, my wife of twelve years went home." He paused, letting go of her hand, and then he suddenly had a questioning look. "Excuse me, but I seem to recognize your voice. In your video blogs, you look like the old-time actress, Audrey Hepburn. Your blog is called, *What Lies Ahead*. I'm a subscriber."

Elmer was staring at them both. "Yes. Now that you mention it, Al, I recognize her voice as well!"

Deborah smiled. "You call him 'Al,' but you said earlier that his name is Zhang Jie." She pronounced the man's Chinese name perfectly.

The man smiled. "'Al' is a nickname I acquired as a teenager, because friends thought I looked like the old-time actor, Al Molinaro. The nickname stuck even while I was attending Liberty University and got my doctorate in Theology. If you wish, you can also call me 'Al.' although you pronounced my name with perfect Chinese enunciation."

"May I call you 'Gee?'"

He smiled broadly. "It will be my honor." He turned to his friend. "I have been on the phone all morning, Elmer. You said moments ago that Deborah is from Long Beach. I have been conversing for several days with a search committee for a large Chinese congregation in the City of Lakewood. Is that not near Long Beach?" He looked at Deborah.

She nodded. "Yes, Lakewood is immediately north of Long Beach. I live in Signal Hill actually, which is surrounded by Long Beach but is a separate city of about two square miles. How are you impressed with the congregation in Lakewood?"

"They have made an attractive offer, but I'm not at all sure I want to accept. At this point I don't feel called there. Elmer, can we discuss this over lunch? I'm getting hungry."

Elmer smiled. "Of course. Deborah, would you like to join us?"

She shook her head. "If you don't mind, I'd like to remain here and pray for a couple of hours."

He nodded. "That'll be fine."

She turned to Gee and opened her purse. "If you go down there to visit, give me a call, and I'd be happy to take you to lunch." She handed him her card. "Here's how to reach me, Gee. Thank you for the lunch invitation, Elmer, but I thrive upon being present to God's presence in prayer. This appears to be a good place to do that. I do my best to serve God on His terms, His way, for His glory. It's been nice to meet both of you."

When the men left, she went to the front of the sanctuary and knelt on the steps. She prayed through much of the afternoon. When Elmer returned from lunch, he saw that she was still there praying, but he did not disturb her. When she finally left, she looked in the church office, but he wasn't there.

The next two days, Deborah had a very enjoyable tour of California's wine country north of the Bay area, but her mind frequently went back to her impressions and prayers at Hilltop Christian Center. She began to wonder if God was calling her to move to the Oakland area.

The rest of the week, Deborah used the BART to take her all over the area. In addition to exploring San Francisco, she spent a day walking on the Berkeley Campus of the University of California. On another day she went through the long tunnel through the hills into Walnut Creek and Concord, where she met some old friends for lunch. On Saturday she flew out of San Francisco International Airport back to Long Beach. It was late afternoon when she backed into her garage on Signal Hill.

Inside, she went straight to her bedroom to drop off her suitcase. Then, after changing into sweats and splashing water on her face, she went into her kitchen to get some things started for dinner. As she started into her great room, she took out her phone and touched a speed-dial button. Pastor Jerry's wife answered. "Hi, Deborah! When did you get home?"

"Hi Pam! I got back less than a half hour ago. I was going to ask Pastor Jerry something, but maybe you can answer a question. Up in Oakland there's a Chinese pastor named Zhang Jie. He is interviewing with a large Chinese congregation in Lakewood to be the pastor. Do you know anything about it?"

"Sure. Jerry and I went to a clergy luncheon there a couple of years ago. It's on Del Amo, west of Lakewood Boulevard. The pastor there must be retiring if your new friend is interviewing to be the pastor. The current pastor founded the church before Jerry and I came to Long Beach. I would guess he's in his eighties at least."

"That's interesting, Pam. The reason why I'm asking is that Gee told me that he's not at all sure that he feels called there, but that since his wife died, he wants to get away from Oakland because of all his memories there. We're still looking for an Associate Pastor, aren't we?"

"True."

"I'd like Pastor Jerry and you to pray about this."

"Absolutely! Most of the candidates we have interviewed have been either too young and inexperienced, or they have been okay but just not a good fit. Would you like to talk with Jerry?"

"Not right now, Pam, but thanks. I've got other calls to make. I'll see you tomorrow."

"Okay, Deborah. Bye."

"Bye." She decided to pray until the food she had in her convection oven was ready. She hadn't even closed her eyes when her phone dinged a call. The screen indicated a call from the Long Beach Airport Marriott Hotel. "Hello?"

"Good evening, Deborah. This is Zhang Jie."

"Gee! It's good to hear from you!" What did you decide?"

"I did not accept their call to be Senior Pastor, Deborah. My flight back to Oakland tomorrow is scheduled for 3:00 PM. Perhaps we can worship together at your church tomorrow."

"That will be excellent, Gee. My church is searching for an Associate Minister. My pastor's name is Jerry. After worship, he might like for us to join him for lunch, along with his wife."

"If we have lunch here at the Marriott, I think that will work. Here in Long Beach, the lines seem shorter for outbound flight than for a many other airports."

"Okay, Gee. I'll pick you up at about 9:30 tomorrow morning. I'll see you then. Bye, Gee."

"Bye, Deborah."

Chapter Twelve
God at Work

Overnight, Deborah slept soundly, and there were no dreams that she could remember the next morning. After reading scriptures and praying, she was ravenously hungry as she got dressed. As she fixed breakfast, she ate an apple while thinking about Pastor Jerry and wondering if Gee was going to be the new Associate Minister at Ximeno Christian Church. Even after eating a waffle, two eggs, and four slices of bacon with her juice and coffee, her mind was still on what might happen at the church that day. She had a sense of anticipation, but she was not sure why.

When they arrived at Ximeno Christian Church, Deborah introduced Gee to all the people that greeted them. The Pastor approached them with his wife. "Good morning! I'm Pastor Jerry, and this is my wife, Pam.

Deborah introduced him. "This is Zhang Jie. Many in Oakland call him Al, but I call him Gee."

Jerry nodded. "I'm glad you can join us this morning. I hope we can have lunch together after church."

Gee nodded, smiling. "My flight back to Oakland is at 2:30, so if we have lunch at the Marriott, lunch will fit in nicely before I have to leave."

Jerry smiled. "Would you be willing to reschedule your flight to Wednesday or Thursday? We will pay all your expenses."

Gee nodded. "I prayed about this possibility last evening. Yes. I will call the Marriott as we go in. Right now, I am looking forward to worship."

Pam smiled. "Excellent! Please sit with Deborah and I during worship." Deborah nodded. Gee took out his phone.

Both women noticed that Gee had a beautiful voice, as he sang in flawless English. Jerry preached on Acts 8:26-28, where Philip the Evangelist met with the Ethiopian Eunuch, baptized him, and mysteriously disappeared. The sermon brought back Deborah's memories of God using her in a similar way under different circumstances.

After Jerry had greeted many people at the end of the worship service, the four of them stood outside in the parking lot. Deborah made an offer. "I think that Gee would enjoy seeing the Queen Mary. I am willing to pay for our lunch, either at Sir Winston's Restaurant and Lounge, or at Chelsea's Chowder if you prefer. I recommend Sir Winston's."

Pam's eyes grew wide. "Jerry and I have wanted to eat there for a long time! Jerry! Let's take up Deborah on her offer!"

Jerry smiled. "How can we say no?"

After they sat down at Sir Winston's, Deborah caught the waiter's eye. "Robert, the four of us are on my tab. After we have our desserts, please compute a 25% tip so that I don't have to take the time to figure it out."

"Yes, Ma'am. Thank you. I will see to your having our best service."

"Jerry, Pam, and Gee, please do not worry about the cost of this meal. Paying for it will be my privilege. My late husband, James, made it possible through his inheritance for us to live well whenever we choose to. I try not to be wasteful, and it will please me if none of you waste this opportunity. Just enjoy whatever you want that is on the menu." Deep within her, Deborah believed that James would enjoy this meal with them if he were there.

Later, as she was signing the chit, she spoke softly to the waiter. "Robert, is there a small lounge where the four of us can meet with some privacy? We have some business to discuss."

"Certainly. "Folks, if you will all follow me, please?"

Robert escorted them to a small lounge about the size of Deborah's great room at her home. They talked and got to know one another for more than two hours.

It was late afternoon when Deborah pulled up in front of the Marriott. "It has been good to start getting to know you, Gee. Tomorrow morning, I need to post to my blog as I always do. Then I have a teleconference with people with whom I've been working since before my husband was killed. Pastor Jerry will pick you up as he has arranged, and then you'll meet with the search committee for lunch and a meeting afterward. If you need to reach me, you have my cell number. Okay?"

Gee nodded. "Yes, Deborah, thank you. Thank you also for a wonderful meal on the Queen Mary. It will be a fond memory. If not before, I'll see you at the worship service on Wednesday."

"Yes, Gee." She nodded. He got out and went inside.

She touched a button on her steering wheel. "Call my parents' home."

"Hi Deborah." Her Mom sounded tired. "Your Dad and I had a nice nap this afternoon. We just woke up."

She put the car in gear. "I hope I didn't wake you up."

"Don't worry about it. If we sleep too long during an afternoon, we don't sleep as well at night. What's going on? Is Gee still with you?"

"No, I just dropped him off. I'm heading home to write and rehearse my blog. Then, after I have a snack, I'll return phone calls to Alice and Jess."

"Hey, Deborah! How's things?" Her Dad sounded as energetic as always.

"I'm doing fine. I just dropped Gee off, and I'll be home in a few minutes. I treated Pastor Jerry, Pam, and Gee to a meal at Sir Winston's on the Queen Mary. Right now, I'm remembering that you two have not eaten there for quite a while. Your anniversary and Easter coincide soon, so maybe I'll take you there for dinner. What do you think?"

"That would be great!" Her Mom almost shouted, and her Dad agreed.

Moments later, Deborah backed into her garage. She had much to do before the Wednesday night worship service. She often missed the mid-week service, but this week she was almost certain that Pastor Jerry would introduce Gee as their new Associate Minister starting next month.

As usual on Wednesday, they began by singing some praise songs. Then pastor Jerry went to the podium with Gee. "Many of you met Zhang Jie last Sunday morning." He turned to Gee. "Did I pronounce that correctly?" Gee nodded. "Deborah Maffett has called him Gee from when she first met him, and the rest of us do to. He's been with us three days now. We started searching for an Associate Minister nearly a year ago, and now Gee has accepted our call, beginning next month."

There was applause from the congregation. Then Jerry continued. "His portfolio for us will reflect his strengths and interests. First, he will share with me in pastoral care and counseling. Second, he will oversee all our Christian education programs. He will be introducing cross-cultural and multi-ethnic emphasis to lead us into the changing population in the Long Beach area. Third, up in Oakland, Gee grew a large youth missions ministry, and he will be doing that here as well. Finally, one or sometimes two Sundays each month he will be preaching."

"Tonight," Jerry continued, "Gee will be preaching from Mark 7:24-30, where a woman from another culture challenges Jesus, and he commends her for it. Gee?"

Jerry stepped off the platform, and Gee began a sermon that turned out to be a brilliant understanding of reaching across cultural and ethnic boundaries.

That night, Deborah was restless, so as she lay in bed, she discussed what Gee had said with God humbly. "Why am I disturbed by that sermon?" Deborah prayed aloud. She finally drifted off to sleep.

Thursday morning after breakfast, Deborah continued to pray about it. She prayed about the sermon while standing, pacing, kneeling, and prostrate on her carpet, but no answers were forthcoming. Finally, she began typing random thoughts on her laptop, and her next blog entry began to take shape. "Okay, Lord, it seems like you've been with me in this struggle over what Gee said Wednesday evening. I'm seeing the Syrophoenician differently than I have before. I'm also seeing your response to her, Lord, a little differently. Please help!" She closed her eyes, but with her eyes closed she was acutely aware of the Lord's presence. She started a new blog document.

> *Most people seem pleased that so much of our political climate in the United States is vastly improved because the past corruption has been confronted, shining light into the darkest corners of our federal and state bureaucracies. Our media are making positive efforts to respond to this refreshed reality.*
>
> *There is a stark contrast between the way Jesus responded to a woman from another ethnic group from His own, and the way our media continue to respond to minorities. Our media continue to exploit the contrasts between ethnic groups to draw attention to themselves with the hope of greater profits. Even if there is no conflict involved, our media want their audiences to seem as though there is conflict.*

For nearly ten minutes, Deborah's *What Lies Ahead* blog cited many examples of the media's exploitation of newsmakers. Even as her blog was being watched for the first time on Friday morning, thousands of supportive responses began flooding in. Over the weekend, the media were pounded again and again.

At 9:00 AM in Long Beach, Deborah began a teleconference with Jethro, Saul, and Fred. "Jethro, we need to begin preparing for the mid-term campaigns that will begin in just a few months."

"Yes. There are some old-establishment people that have held on despite the confrontations. Some of them will need to be confronted with additional embarrassments. We can keep up the pressure upon them. Saul?"

"As I look over our list, I think that over the next month or so, at least half of them will not be running again. If they do, the media are going to hammer them like never before."

Fred nodded. "Yes. This time there won't be very many that we will have to confront, but we must be ready for the new people on the political horizon. Since they don't have political background recorded, we are going to have to dig deeper into their personal histories."

"Agreed." Saul was adamant. "It's going to be harder for some of these new people."

Jethro was thoughtful. "Fred, when your crew was going through Maddy Schmitt's gossip siftings, did you learn anything about her methods?"

Fred shook his head. "Not really. She seemed to have insights that came out of her personal gifts. Saul, have you analyzed Maddy Schmitt's techniques for sifting out the truth?"

"No, but you've made a valid point, Jethro. I'll analyze her techniques. If we can sift out some methodology from her, we can apply those methods to the gossip columns written about the new politicians. Also, if any of them majored in political science in university work, we can learn about them from the papers they have written. Why don't you and your crew, Fred, pursue that angle."

"Okay."

During this dialog, Deborah was praying. She opened her eyes to her laptop camera. "Fred, those term papers written for political science classes are important. Also, we can be sure to glean additional insights about them from articles they have written for their college papers, both digital and in print."

Fred nodded. "Okay."

Deborah continued. "I have a connection with the Schmitt family, Jethro. Depending upon how I approach Maddy, I might be able to recruit her as sort of an adjunct consultant to our team."

Saul nodded. "You can approach her as the *What Lies Ahead* blogger and not identify yourself personally. Jethro, I suggest that you reach out to her on Deborah's behalf with one of your super-secure emails."

Now, Jethro nodded. "I'll reach out to her in the same way that God helped Deborah reach out to me the first time, by way of Mars."

"**Mars**?" Saul almost exploded with surprise. "Someday, my friend, you'll have to explain that one to me, but not today."

Jethro chuckled. "Okay. Someday."

Deborah interjected. "Enough for today, guys. Jethro, as soon as you get a response from Maddy, let me know. Bye for today, everyone."

Less than an hour later, Deborah's phone rang with a call from Jethro. "Hey. I put on my John Wayne mask and voice modifier, and I made a video call to Maddy. I knew she was in her apartment by herself, and she was electronically isolated as I called. I asked her if she would be interested in helping the blogger of *What Lies Ahead* with sifting through gossip in state capitals. She gave me an enthusiastic yes that I think was honest. She's a fan of yours, without a doubt. She has posted dozens of supportive posts to your blog. You can read them if you want to, using that special search engine I gave you."

"Okay, so what's next, do you think?"

"I told her that if she is electronically silent between now and 9:00 PM Eastern Time, the blogger will make a video call to her laptop. That's you. That's 6:00 PM Pacific time. Be sure to wear your mask and have a special background. The secure phone number I've created for her is now in your directory of contacts."

"Okay, thanks. Say hello to Alice for me. This coming Sunday afternoon, I'd like you both to come over here to my place. In addition to visiting, I want Alice to help me put some German satire into my Monday morning blog post."

"Okay, see you then. Meantime, let me know how things go with Maddy."

"Right. Bye." She ended the connection. She looked out the window and prayed aloud. "Lord, Jethro thinks Maddy is worthy of our trust, and maybe she is, but does she have a friend, perhaps a close friend, who could betray our trust. I trust Jethro, Lord, but I trust You more, and with everything." She closed her eyes.

It was after 5:00 o'clock when Deborah changed her clothes and put on her mask. She set up the call in front of a chromakey green wall and digitally inserted a video image of the Lincoln Memorial as a background. At 6:00 she made the connection. "Good evening, Maddy. It's good to meet you."

"I'm delighted to meet you, Ma'am. You look like Audrey Hepburn. Should I call you Audrey?"

"Let's use the name Deborah for this call. I am part of a team that has been working against political corruption, as you know. Not long ago I discovered that you were helping some of Washington's Senators clean up corruption. Evidently you have some excellent instincts for sorting out the truth out of gossip. Is that a fair analysis of what you have been doing?"

She nodded. "Yes, Ma'am. – Deborah. Hacker Dude tells me that you want me to do some similar analysis at the state level."

"Yes, Maddy, and you will be paid for your efforts."

"I do it free for my uncle."

"I know, Maddy, but this may be a bigger challenge and more time consuming. If you agree to do it, Hacker Dude will supply you with URLs to the gossip pages of hundreds of newspapers." Deborah paused. "There's something else, Maddy."

"What's that?"

"There's a woman about your age that you consider a trustworthy friend. She will betray you if paid enough. If you put your mind to it, you know who I'm talking about. I'm telling you this because you need to be more cautious with this larger project. Do you want to do it?"

"Yes. Definitely. I will do my best."

"Good. Since tomorrow is the first day of the month, I will pay you monthly from now on. I will wire transfer an advance into your checking account immediately. It will come from a law firm in Southern California. Create a directory on the 'C' drive of your computer named 'Hackerdude,' all one word. I suggest you create a sub-directory for each politician whose gossip you're analyzing."

"I do that anyway."

"Okay. I'll check in with you from time to time. We're interested in anything you get on those running for major office for the midterms. If I want to use you again after that, I'll let you know. Do you have any questions, Maddy?"

"No Ma'am."

"Good. Bye, Maddy." Deborah ended the call." Her phone immediately rang, showing Jethro as the caller. "Hi, Jethro. Did you listen in?"

"How did you know?"

"We know each other, Jethro."

"That we do. That was a nice touch, telling her to create a directory called 'hackerdude.'"

"There was no point in freaking her out by telling her that you already have a mirror copy her entire hard drive that is constantly updated. I suggest that we monitor all of her communications until we are confident that we can trust her."

"I'm also going to be monitoring that so-called 'friend' of hers named Tricia. I don't think Maddy suspects her yet, but now that you've warned her, she might figure it out."

This pleased Deborah. "How soon will you give her the URLs of gossip pages we need to watch?"

"I'm still compiling the list. It's amazing how readily these columnists rate each other."

"There's an old saying that goes, 'Those willing to gossip with you will also be willing to gossip about you.' It's no wonder that the Bible so consistently identifies gossip with sin and with evil. Let's touch bases again in a few days, Jethro."

"Right. Bye." He ended the call."

Deborah went to her master bathroom to remove her mask and change her clothes.

Chapter Thirteen
Midterms & Surprises

Jethro's weekly blog, *A Hacker's Hopes*, was getting harder to write. On New Year's Eve, he found it somewhat easier.

> *It is good to see people truly prepared to celebrate New Year's Eve again. Tomorrow is the first day of a New Year and it is the first day of a year of mid-term election campaigns. This hacker hopes that most of the corrupt politicians that have held on to their offices despite embarrassing revelations will not run again. History needs to have their replacements outshine them brilliantly.*

In a friendly satire, Jethro suggested some things that might be accomplished by those elected to replace incumbents. Then, without mentioning any failures by the media, he offered praise for the best journalism by a media outlet.

> *I have no influence regarding the Pulitzer Prizes given out each year, but I hope that recognition be offered to the UBN network, or at least to some of its reporters. The network has consistently been accurate and properly focused. When I have submitted to be interviewed, the network has been more than fair.*

Deborah called him the next morning. "I'm glad you gave some recognition to UBN in your blog. I would not be surprised if Nicholas Terry gets one of the prizes."

"I agree. By the way, Maddy has hardly communicated with her questionable friend. Have you noticed how many people she has anticipated running for office? Most of them have been candidates for state offices, but a few have been for President Peterson's bureaucratic replacements that have been easily confirmed by the senate. Maddy has become a real asset to the team."

In February, a few weeks later in one of their weekly teleconferences, Saul raised a similar point. "I am glad we decided to avail ourselves of the expertise of Maddy Schmitt. Her gifts are unique, and her results are useful to us. I don't know how the rest of you feel, but I would personally welcome her at these teleconferences of ours."

Deborah nodded. "I'll pray about it, Saul. I've toyed with that idea in the back of my mind anyway. Fred, what do you think?"

"The people that she has raised as possible good candidates have been simple to check out for basic coverage, and when those people have announced their candidacies, we were ready to follow through more easily. Jethro, what do you say?"

"I've thought about that possibility from the beginning, but I want to wait until Deborah follows through to see what the Lord says."

That night, Deborah had a vivid dream, and the next morning, she put on her mask and called Maddy. After initial greetings, Deborah told her the reason for the call. "Maddy, you have been extremely helpful with what you have put into your hackerdude directory."

"Thanks! I'm glad to hear it."

"Hackerdude and I are the leaders of a team that has produced the emails targeting our political establishment. After much prayer, it has been decided to make your participation in our efforts more complete. This means two things. First, we hold a weekly teleconference that is secured by hackerdude. These are held at 9:00 AM Pacific Time, usually on Monday mornings. One member of the team lives in Ohio, one lives in Florida, and hackerdude and I live in Southern California. The meetings will be at noon your time, so you'll have to block out at least an hour at noon every Monday. Usually, the meetings are less than that, but they have run longer a few times."

"Okay. I'm glad you mentioned prayer because it is important to my whole family. What's the other thing?"

"You've been able to stay under the radar until now, but with becoming part of our team, we have to beef up security for you."

"Really! I've never felt like I'm in any danger."

"Your digital security was beefed up several months ago. Now there will be some undercover operatives nearby wherever you go. They may not have to introduce themselves, but if you feel like you're being followed, just mention it to me and I'll check it out. If the person following you is not one of our operatives, you'll have reassurance. Now, before your first meeting with us on Monday, let me tell you about the others."

After telling Maddy about the rest of the team, she called General Plummer and confirmed Maddy's security detail. Deborah knew that adding Maddy to the team was the right thing to do. Coverage of the mid-term elections was going to go smoothly.

When Maddy was introduced to the team on Monday, Jethro identified himself as Hackerdude, and Deborah did not wear her mask either. Then they got down to business. Maddy's first report was important. "This afternoon, Robert Lassiter will announce in Spokane that he is running for Governor of Washington. My source on this is solid. I've already introduced him previously."

Fred nodded. "Yes. We have copies of editorials he wrote for the student paper when he was a grad student, and we've downloaded a research paper he wrote exposing corruption in Seattle's political machine. We'll post some good material on him on Wednesday. He's pretty clean, isn't he Jethro?"

"Yes. When our President was still governor of Oregon, he introduced her at a student forum, and she has nurtured friendship with him. He's solid."

To Maddy's relief, the teleconference lasted just under an hour. She was starving when it ended, and she headed towards *BLT Steak* to meet with her Dad, Senator Hans Schmitt, for lunch. As usual, she wore two video recorders mounted in hair clips on her head. A few months earlier, Jethro had arranged for electronic jammers to be hidden at *BLT Steak* to provide security for those hair clips. Maddy knew nothing about it, and neither did the owners of the restaurant.

Five years earlier, Maddy had a boyfriend who was a student at M.I.T., where she was also finishing her doctorate. He created software for her that would take the recordings from the hairclips, screen out voices selected by Maddy, along with background noise. It then created compiled videos of various people eating in the restaurant that Maddy selected. Her former boyfriend had since gotten married, and Maddy was one of the bridesmaids at the wedding.

When Maddy got home from having lunch with her Dad, she followed her afternoon routine. This time, Maddy was able to put three new files in her Hackerdude directory. Less than a half-hour later, Jethro called her. "Hey Maddy, did you make these new videos at lunch today?"

"Yes. I had lunch with my Dad at *BLT Steak.*"

"I take it you wore those special hair clips of yours."

"So, you know about them. I'm not surprised. My software filters out my voice, my Dad's voice and the background noise. Then, all I must do is focus on the conversations that I think are useful. A long time ago, I asked my Dad if learned useful things electronically when we had lunch together, should I tell him. He thought about a moment, and then he said no. He trusts me, and what he didn't know about he didn't have to keep secret."

"You're Dad is a brilliant man, Maddy."

"I know. Will Fred's crew go over what I've submitted?"

"That's right. They will probably send a note to Saul to call his attention to the pork being inserted in that one bill."

"Why?"

"When we were confronting corruption, we often used pork as ammunition in our confrontation emails. This time around, we want to place primary focus on being supportive of clean politics over unnecessary pork. Our focus is a little different. In my blog next Monday, I may offer some satire on political pork."

"I understand. Is there anything else we need to talk about?"

"Not right now. We may talk later this week. Bye, Maddy."

"Bye, Jethro."

Alice was sitting next to him in their home in the Palos Verdes Estates. She took off her earphones. "That's a good idea, my love, talking about pork in your next blog."

Jethro shook his head. "I don't know if I can deal with pork without coming across to negative or without inviting too many negative responses."

Alice smiled. "Did you ever watch any episodes of the old television series, *The West Wing*?"

"Sure! That was a great show! I binge watched it when I was in high school."

"There's an episode where the administration is supportive of a health care bill, where they don't allow one old senator to add an item that they saw as pork. The senator started a filibuster."

"I remember that. The addition to the bill that he wanted was not about adding pork but about his grandson, who had a tragic disease." Jethro paused. "I see your point. I can use that example of how many things are necessary, but in a bill about to go to the Senate floor, etc. etc."

Alice smiled. "Then you can say that what they want is not like an egregious example of pork, but, and then we can insert some satire."

"Right. Let's keep this in mind and pray about it before writing my next blog post next Sunday. The mid-term primaries are coming up in a few months."

"Yes, and our son is due to be born this summer. Those first few weeks I won't be able to help you much, but by late September, things may stabilize some. I talked with Jess yesterday. Her due date is just two days after ours. Saul inserted a comment into the conversation, saying that he thinks she has become the sexiest woman on the planet."

Jethro laughed. "I could say the same about you, my glorious wife!"

Epilog
Loose Ends

Alice and Jethro Underwood named their son Elisha ("Eli"). Eli was born in Seaside Hospital in Long Beach. Four days later, Jess and Saul Wolfe welcomed a daughter into their life at TriPoint Medical Center. They named her Ruth.

Senator Hans Schmitt and his wife began to think that Maddy would never get married, but when they invited her to dinner to celebrate her thirty-eighth birthday, she brought her fiancé, Dennis Batten, and they announced that they would get married at Lake Tahoe the following June.

Fred Drake's wife of 32 years died of breast cancer. He was so devasted he shut down his business for almost seven months. Then he went to a sunrise Easter service at Bathtub Beach, and on impulse at the end of the service, he asked the pastor to baptize him. As he came up out of the water, he felt like he started a new life.

Walking away from the water towards the parking area, a woman who was walking nearby said, "I'm sure glad I finally got baptized like Jesus did today. I put it off for years. How about you? I'm Dixie, by the way."

Fred looked at her and smiled. "I'm Fred Drake. When my wife died of breast cancer seven months ago, I think my faith faltered. I didn't want to go to church and see so many people who I associated with my wife. This morning, I got re-baptized, sort of to start fresh and re-connect with Jesus. That may not be a valid reason, but that's why I did it. I feel like I'm a new man."

He reached his car and stopped. "I'm headed out to breakfast at *Berry Fresh*. Would you like to join me?"

She smiled. "I was headed there anyway. Sure!"

The following November, on the Sunday afternoon before Thanksgiving, Dixie and Fred got married at Bathtub Beach, where they had met. He was fifty-one, and she was thirty-one.

Deborah's entire team was there with their children. Jess was pregnant again, and so was Alice.

Jess and Saul's daughter, Ruth, wanted to go to the office with Saul as she started going to Kindergarten. She asked him questions about cases he was working on that challenged him to look at situations differently. By the time she turned ten, she was part of the teleconferences held by Deborah and Jethro whenever the conferences were held.

Alice and Jethro's son, Eli, was watching Jethro work at his computer as soon as he could walk. By the time he entered school, Jethro and Alice were quite sure that Eli was smarter than his father. He wrote his first program while in the third grade.

Former President John Dough remained repentant. After he renewed his faith in Jesus, he led the rest of his family towards being faithful followers of Jesus.

Deborah did not re-marry. Just after turning fifty-four, she adopted four children at Ximeno Christian Church when their parents were killed in an auto accident. George and Alexandra Zuniga were delighted to have the two boys and two girls as their grandchildren. The oldest, a thirteen-year-old boy named Mike, joined Deborah and Jethro's team when God started giving him dreams, and she had him start helping her write her blog posts. Mike became a prophet.

Corruption in Washington D.C. and most of the state capitols was minimal for more than three generations, stretching Deborah's prophecy....

Other Books by James J. Stewart
Only Available on Amazon

Christian Inspiration, Study, and Poetry

Brief Prayers for Your Church Community
[366 brief prayers]

Faith and Yosemite: Fourth Edition
[Christian poetry with pictures of Yosemite]

Faith Fuel
[Meditations on the Christian faith and life]

Lasting Love
[Short Biographical Sketches]

Living for Jesus
[A Gospels Study Guide for Couples and Small Groups]

Deliberately Growing Spiritually
[A five-year Bible reading program for spiritual transformation.]

Seed Thoughts for Christian Prayer and Meditation
[Workbook]

Single Sentence Sermons
[Workbook for growing faith]

Walking in Faith
[Much of the same poetry as Faith and Yosemite but without pictures]

Spiritually Growing Through Prayer
The focus is upon personal piety and spiritual growth through prayer.

In Jesus' Name
[Praying Effectively]

Christian Fiction

A Man, A Woman and a Cat
[A cheetah/Puma crossbreed brings together an architect and actress.]

A Marriage of Miracles
[God sets up a romance for two people's miracles]

The Camera Doctors
[Two people meeting on a mountain leads to romance]

Casting Lots
[Christian romance set in the near future]

Christian Romances in the Foothills
An anthology of Tom's Town, Soul Mates, & The Camera Doctors

An Extensive Life
[The life story of a man who lived 400 years.]

Elijah
God gives a modern prophet dreams for his blog.

Empty Tomb, Full Hearts
[Testimonies of some who Saw the Risen Christ]

The First Lady
[A couple stumble into politics and make history.

The Gaardian Saga
[Christian science fiction fantasy involving God]

God, Love, and Stargazing
God prepares two people for romance and service.

A Nation Transformed
[A tale of God intervening in the USA with miracles.

A Second Call to Serve
[A pastor and his second wife build a church from scratch.]

Prayer Warriors
A continuation of Casting Lots]

Soul Mates
[Romance in the same setting as Tom's Town]

This World Is Not My Home
[Two people separate to find love with others.]

Tom's Town
[Small town life and Christian romance]

The Warrior and the Prophet
[God has surprises and blessings for newlyweds]

Yosemite Picture Books

Ever-Changing Yosemite Valley
*[Yosemite Valley is a glacially carved valley.
Moment by moment, scenes change.]*

Faith and Yosemite Fourth Edition
*[Pictures of Yosemite National Park,
with poems about the Christian faith]*

Portraits of El Capitan
[El Capitan rises 3000 feet above the floor of Yosemite Valley]

Portraits of Half Dome
[Half Dome marks the east end of Yosemite Valley]

A Sense of Wonder: Yosemite
[A Christian poem about Yosemite, illustrated with pictures]

Starlight Over Yosemite
[Large pictures of Yosemite taken at night]

Yosemite Textures and Shadows
*[High-definition photographs of Yosemite Valley,
depicting all seasons, both day and night.]*